"HEY MOM, THE RECLINER FELL ON DAD AGAIN!"

Tom McKenna

Dedication

This is dedicated… to the one I love…Betty Ann
also, to Georgie… My brother, my inspiration and my best friend.

Acknowledgement

Many thanks to Carolyn V. Hamilton of Swift House Press whose invaluable editorial oversight and skills helped make this book possible. Ms. Hamilton is an Author, Editor and Writing Coach who can be reached at info@swifthousepress.com.

Table of Contents

Dedication iii

Acknowledgement v

Erma, Art, Neil & Me 1

Exile On Vain Street 7

"Hey Mom, The Recliner Fell On Dad Again!" 20

Silent Cal, The Big Train & The '24 Senators 27

Epilogue 40

Dance Of The Deacon 44

Confessions Of A Non-Best-Selling Author 91

Erma, Art, Neil & Me

Well, it certainly started innocently enough. I was reading my emails, nonchalantly deleting the gazillion Groupon notifications populating my inbox, when a new message appeared. Shubert Haus was holding its next short story competition. They were calling on all writers to submit their absolute best stories, to essentially inspire, entertain and tantalize every fiber of the literary senses. Those sitting in judgment would be awarding its most prestigious award in American humor to one deserving honoree.

Inspire, entertain and tantalize? That left me out. Or did it? After taking a quick mental inventory assessing my abilities to fulfill such criteria, I had my fair share of self-doubt and rightfully so. Trepidations aside, wasn't it true that during my career in the private sector, I inspired a few of my subordinates to become supervisors like me? Was it because I possessed some innate leadership quality they saw within me, or was it because they felt if I could perform the job, anyone could? If it please the court your honor, I would at this time, like to invoke my Fifth Amendment rights.

Entertain? Well, I did get a lot of high fives at work the day after the annual company picnic. After all, how hard can it be to transpose one-liners and a few pratfalls in front of tipsy co-workers into award winning prose? Tantalize? Okay, we are definitely going to have to settle for two out of three here, although even that may be a stretch. But what are writers, if not fearless warmongers willing to do battle with the written word at every chance they get?

Isn't their penchant for soul-baring confessions and "leaving it all on the floor" fulfilling enough? And now, that fortress of funny, that sanctuary of the sublime, that palace of purple-free prose, the Shubert Haus was putting out an APB to all those so inclined.

I decided I was all in, but not before first paying a visit to the shrines of my patron saints of highbrow humor. Hopefully, I would derive all the graces and merits necessary to inspire and elevate my game to stratospheric heights. I would also invoke my benefactors to protect me from the sins of misspellings and the evils of grammatical errors. I walked into my den and over to the giant bookcase that housed my heros' acclaimed earthly works and scanned the shelves.

There they were, like silent sentries guarding their tomes. Erma Bombeck: high priestess of humility and the self-deprecating art form. Art Buchwald: syndicated columnist and political pundit whose acerbic wit and scathing parodies skewered Democrats and Republicans alike; but whose civility has not been seen since. Neil Simon: the template for the modern playwright, who gracefully juxtaposed madcap comedies with urbane sophistication.

The holy trinity of all things funny.

I picked up my well-worn copy of Erma's classic, *If Life is a Bowl of Cherries, What am I Doing in the Pits?* and started leafing through it, hoping to glean a scintilla of Erma's droll writing style. As I turned to replace the book to the shelf, my shoulder inadvertently struck the case hard enough to knock over my entire DVD box set collection of *Hee Haw* from Time Life. My last memory after being conked on the head, prior to blacking out, was of Grandpa Jones and Junior Samples coming at me with pitchforks.

A few moments later, I had somewhat of an out-of-body experience. I saw myself lying on the floor, seeing stars and birdies flying in small tight orbits around my head. I saw myself hunching my elbows up under my body, high enough to support myself. I vigorously shook my jowls back and forth to revive myself, like I had seen numerous times on cartoon shows. I was now in a place that emanated light, truth and a lot of patchy ground fog. I heard a small commotion and turned to my left to see the trio of Bombeck, Buchwald and Simon talking and bickering amongst themselves.

Erma was adjusting her halo and eating tortilla chips with avocado dip when she turned to me and said, "Hey kid, you okay? You gave us quite a start there for a moment."

"I'm fine," I replied, more embarrassed over my clumsiness than anything else. "Where am I?" I asked no one in particular.

Art, clad in a toga with a laurel on his head, lounging on a daybed and holding a small sprig of grapes over his mouth, answered. "You're right where you want to be, kid. You're in the presence of greatness, and we are here to help you out."

"But how did you know I was looking for help?" I cried.

Neil, fiddling with a broken comedy/tragedy mask, seemed annoyed at my impertinence and snapped, "Come on, kid, I'm from Yonkers, not Peoria. Besides, I've got a golf date with Lemmon, Matthau and Mel Brooks and my tee time's at 3 p.m."

"But Mel Brooks isn't dead," I protested.

"Yeah, but it's not 3 p.m. yet either," Neil shot back. "Besides, it's your wacky dream, so let's get this crazy train rolling."

Erma turned to me and asked, "Does this robe make me look fat?

Maybe wearing a rope belt will help." "Ah…no," I hesitated. "You look…fine!"

"You're no different from these other two slackers," Erma chided. "But never mind. What have you got for me? How may I help you with your writing?"

"What are the most important elements in writing a funny story?" I queried.

"Always start with a great beginning, a memorable middle and always go out with a bang. Secondly, employ self-deprecating humor. Audiences love feeling smarter than you. And thirdly, exaggerate,

exaggerate, exaggerate. I never should have had this avocado dip. My ankles are going to swell up the size of ostrich eggs by morning. You get the idea kid?"

Before I could reply, Erma had a question for me.

"Why are all the young bucks today wearing earrings and cinnamon rolls on top of their heads?"

"I think the earring trend comes from a string of successful pirate movies that Johnny Depp made. The cinnamon rolls are actually real hair tied back in what's known as the man bun. They are extremely popular, and according to the dudes, very versatile, too."

At this juncture, Art was eating Erma's chips and spilling the avocado dip on his yellow plaid tie.

"Alright Sparky, how can I help you out? Hit me!" Art barked.

"Mr. Buchwald," I said, "How do I learn to write hard-hitting, biting satire?"

"First and foremost, know your subject inside out. Dip your quill into the inkwell of mockery and sarcasm and then cut them off at the knees. It's like J.R. Ewing of *Dallas* used to profess. Once you get past your conscience, the rest is easy. I got one for you now, rookie. With all the space junk floating around up here and smog being what it is, I have a tough time following politics. Who's the Governor of California now, and how's he doing?"

"That would be Governor Jerry Brown, sir," I replied.

Art started to choke on a tortilla chip and gasped, "The same Jerry Brown who was governor in the early eighties? That must have been over thirty years ago! What's he been doing lately?"

"Well," I said, "he passed legislation recently making the possession of plastic straws a criminal offense. On the flip side, he legalized marijuana in his state last year."

"And the President of the United States? Did Clinton's boy, Al Gore ever make it to the White House?" Art asked.

"No," I said. "Gore lost the election to George W. Bush in a nail biter by a few buckets of hanging chads in Florida. But don't feel too sorry for Al, because he went on to invent the Internet, and after that Global Warming, which is basically what the name implies."

"So, who's the president today?" Art demanded. "Donald Trump," I said.

"The pig farmer in Boise, Idaho, Donald Trump?" Art asked. "Or the real estate tycoon from Manhattan, Donald Trump?"

"The one from New York," I said.

"Well, how's he doing?" Art spat. "What does the public think of him?" "Half the population refers to him as Hitler, and the other half calls him a messiah. I like to think of him as a little bit of both."

Neil seemed to be getting a little antsy and was adjusting his comedy/tragedy mask over his face. "Shubert Haus Contest, huh kid? Jeez, you got your work cut out for you. Cripes, I've *never* even copped a writing award from them. Go ahead, fire away!"

"Mr. Simon, how do I develop characters who are compelling, emotionally driven, and possess a bittersweet sense of purpose?" "Take a writing class!" Neil responded.

"It's too late!" I cried. "The contest closes in two weeks."

"Listen, rook," Neil said, "There are over one hundred and fifty thousand words in Webster's dictionary. Your task is to find the perfect word combinations and put them in sequential order, so they are in a concise, intelligible and entertaining format, of award-winning caliber. Sooo…what's the issue again?"

Before I could respond, Erma glanced over at Art who was now eating a sausage pizza, and took it upon herself to come to my defense. "Nice going Neil, nothing like killing the dream," she scolded.

"Damn Erma, I just want the kid to realize that it's hard work, and no one can do it for him. Did I ever tell you I had to do twenty re-writes of *Come Blow Your Horn* before it got on Broadway?"

"Yeah, Neil, you told me, like…twenty times," Erma said.

While this was going on, Art and I were talking sports, baseball in particular. I told Art how the Red Sox finally broke their eighty-six-year-old curse by sweeping the Cards in '04.

"Come on kid, give me some dirt. I knew all that," Art whined.

"How about the Cubs?" I countered. "Did you know they snagged their first series crown since 1908, by downing the Indians in 2016?"

"Yep," Art said. "I don't have many connections left on earth, but luckily, Vin Scully of the Dodgers still takes my calls."

Erma, Art and Neil came closer to me and asked me if I had any more questions for them. When I said no, they gave me hugs and handshakes and wished me luck. Erma said she was either going to go to the gym or the bakery.

Art mentioned that he still had a deadline to bang out for the *Pearly Gates Gazette,* and Neil stated that he was headed off to hit a pail of balls at the driving range before his golf date.

I asked Neil what it was like golfing with Lemmon and Matthau.

Neil let out a long sigh and said, "Jack can be a real pain in the keister. Every time I beat him, he starts whining about all these imaginary ailments that messed up his game. Walter, on the other hand, is the only guy I know who spends more time in the woods than the fairways, and has yet to lose a single ball."

Before they turned to leave, I thanked them all for their advice and support and asked them if they had any questions for me. They looked at one another for a few seconds before Art stepped forward and said, "Just one question, Chief. What in the world are *buckets of hanging chads?*"

Exile On Vain Street

"Ding, ding, ding!" I crushed out another Newport in the hospital's medical records break room, to make my first round of deliveries to the various clinics that St. James Hospital served. In addition to medical records, the ground floor housed the main reception area, the E/R, a blood lab, a Public Safety Office, a small cafeteria and an even smaller chapel. If you turned to your right, exiting the record room, you were directed by a canary yellow arrow on the tiled floor to the pharmacy. This slanted down into a basement floor which morphed into a cavernous labyrinth, housing the mailroom, the boiler room and all the maintenance shops.

St. James Hospital is located dead center on Boston's Harrison Avenue, adjacent to the theatre district. Its medical existence spans over a hundred and seventy-five years, and it has a reputation as a world-renowned teaching hospital.

Over the years its medical professionals have included some of the leading pioneers in their fields, covering everything from early child development to the treatment of childhood illnesses and diseases.

As far as I was concerned, the five-to-one female-to-male employee ratio was its most endearing quality. One month past my high school graduation, I was now gainfully employed as a full-time hospital messenger. The money at the time was meager, but sufficient to keep me in pocket money for all the usual items an eighteen-year-old would require: beer, cigarettes and car expenses.

I suppose it could have been worse. I could have been exiled with the other slopeheads to the mailroom. It was a dank, dreary existence, sorting mail all day, unaware of any changing weather patterns due to the windowless confines of a subterranean work station.

"Mr. McCauley, can you get these records out of here?" Mrs. Jablonski barked.

"I don't want any patients croaking on my watch today."

"On my way, Mrs. J. Anything else before I go?" I asked.

"Yes, swing by the caf on your way back and get me a lemon-raspberry Danish and a small coffee, three sugars, no cream! I'm watching my weight. I'll take care of you when you get back, dear," she said dismissively.

Mrs. Jablonski was the manager of the record room and as such, a sixty- something dynamo who possessed the girth of Sophie Tucker and the brassiness of Ethel Merman. She could out-drink, out-think and out-sing any man or woman alive. Her personality was as over-sized as her Hawaiian muumuus. She could swear like a stevedore and had the temper of a teamster in a non-union shop. Mrs. J. didn't suffer slackers gladly either. Her credo was, "If you can't fire-up your employees with enthusism, then fire them with enthusism!" These attributes notwithstanding, Mrs. J. was a peach.

I loaded up my cart and traversed the clinics starting at the E/R, before blowing through Pediatrics, E.N.T. and a few more, ending half an hour later at Ob/Gyn. Before returning to my home base, I had a final drop- off/pick-up, at the Medical Transcriptions Unit. This department was the counterpart to my office and was used to transcribe all the doctor's medical entries into the records, with the assistance of nearly a dozen young women doing the grunt work.

One of these fine office girls was Ginny Hockley. Ginny had to be one of the cutest little units I had ever laid eyes on. She had detergent-smooth skin with a lion's mane of glossy black hair that seemed to shimmer even on sunless days.

She had soft, liquid brown, bedroom eyes and a tiny baby finger that I surmised could manipulate any dude in its orbit. Unfortunately for me, I wasn't in this sphere, rendering my undying crush on her... unrequited.

I had spied Ginny on a few occasions, flirting outlandishly with a new hire in the blood lab, who I might add, bore an uncanny resemblance to a bloke named Mick Jagger. His composition consisted of pale blue eyes, a mousey brown shag, oversized lips and the requisite hand-on-hip pose whenever some cute young thing chatted him up outside his lab.

On top of these fortuitous traits, his performance of duties permitted him to don a physician's white lab coat over the obligatory blue or green scrubs. This gave him the added cachet of appearing as "Mick Jagger, M.D." all the while making his rounds with a delivery cart full of vials of blood. It was a singular rock star brainiac cocktail that no woman would ever be able to resist.

To enhance his identity even more closely to the iconic frontman, he claimed his name was Nick Sagger, with two g's. He even insisted that everyone use his full moniker when addressing him, as in, "Good morning, Nick Sagger! Did you happen to catch last night's Red Sox score?"

Skeptical, as was my wont, I went so far as to try and have his background information verified at Personnel. H.R. however, was kind enough to remind me that his private information was none of my business. Such data would never be disseminated under legal and/or moral grounds, especially to hospital messengers.

As I pushed my cart towards Ginny's desk to drop and pick up the records, I could feel my palms getting clammy, just from being in her proximity.

"Good morning, Tommy. What's up?" she purred.

"Nothing, Ginny. What's up with you?" I gamely replied.

"Nick Sagger is taking me to see the Stones tonight. Loge seats too," she gushed.

"Aren't you afraid everyone will mistake your date for the genuine article and mob you guys?" I sarcastically quipped.

"We'll take our chances. Did you ever get your tickets?" she parried nonchalantly.

"Yeah, I'm going tomorrow night with some friends and my kid sister," I blurted.

"Your kid sister? That should be fun," she stated without a trace of ambiguity.

I dismissed her last comment, said hello to a few of the other girls, completed my records swap and headed to the caf for Mrs. J's order.

The rest of the day flew by as I thought that in less than thirty-six hours, I would see the Rolling Stones for my first time.

As excited as I was to see the lads and to hear their canon of classics that the band had been churning out for the past seven or eight years, my relationship with my rock gods could at times leave me feeling somewhat ambivalent. Of course, it was never anything major. I just thought that sometimes the Stones' publicity machine went overboard when it came to selling the band. I never understood how they could get away with portraying the boys as these filthy, vile, uncouth thugs, when I viewed the lot of them as creampuffs.

Well, perhaps not Richards, who I heard, once planted his boot squarely in the face of some pug-ugly during one of their early Scottish dates. By Keith's account, the lout had it coming for spitting at him on stage. Whenever early photo-ops of the boys cropped up, you'd have thought them a mere quintet of Westminster Abbey choirboys, outfitted by Savile Row. Certainly not a scrum of dirty, ill-mannered ruffians, run afoul of the queen. More recently, even Mick's song lyrics had given me pause to consider some of the things he was spouting. Just from reading about his vigorous workout regimen, I knew he wasn't a monkey, and I definitely knew all his friends weren't junkies. Not unless you consider Truman, Bianca and Andy yachting in the south of France, sipping Bordeaux and mimosas as hard drug activity.

And please, Mick, don't call me out for taking out Jack and Bobby when I was nowhere near Dealey Plaza or the Ambassador Hotel on those fateful days. Minor grievances aside, this was their first American tour in three years, since the tragic disaster at Altamont in December '69. Having seen *Gimme Shelter* some half dozen times, it still cut like a two-edged sword. Despite the senseless violence of the event, the mystique and popularity surrounding the band only seemed to heighten their status in the pantheon of rock's highest echelon.

Three years as a dormant touring band had made them much more in demand. And with the Beatles having thrown in the towel two year's prior, the Stones had a clear path to the throne known as the world's greatest rock and roll band.

Sure, Zeppelin and The Who lurked in the weeds, but by the summer of '72, the Stones had a greater body of work. Plus, they were touring in support of their latest *Exile* album, which already had a handful of hits climbing up *Billboard's Top 100*.

When I got home from work, I called my best friend Buzzy De'Coste to go over final arrangements for the concert the following night. Buzzy and I went back to the fourth grade. Guys like Buzzy were a dime a dozen. He was average at sports and academics, but always knew the locations of all the cool weekend parties. He was the only guy I knew who could drive a stick shift and roll a joint at the same time. Despite these lofty credentials, Buzzy wasn't above ripping off your pot if he suspected you were sufficiently passed out at a house party. Buzzy was cool as long as you took him at face value.

Anyways, Buzzy was also taking his girlfriend of two months, Sudsy Simpson to the show. Her real name was Karen. I never got the details, but for whatever reason, she was forever known as

"Sudsy" after attending a party last winter in the company of another girl, and the entire offensive line of the local high school football team.

Two months earlier, Buzzy and I had listened to the special announcement on the radio which specified all the mailing instructions in order to secure our Stones tickets. We were tasked with mailing a check or money order, in the amount of twenty-four dollars for the four-ticket maximum, to some obscure post office box in N.Y.C. The ticket request had to be postmarked no earlier than May 15th and no later than May 16th.

I figured all the cloak-and-dagger secrecy involving the ticket agency was generated because they simply didn't want the hassle of having to return a gazillion orders for seats that were already filled. Maybe Jagger wasn't the only one who had attended the London School of Economics.

Buzzy and I took his '67 Mustang over to the South Postal Annex on the 15th to mail our requests. When we arrived at the postal docks where the trailer trucks were pulling in and out, we chanced upon a clerk who was taking a smoke break and asked him if he could put our letter in the mail stream. Like an animatronic figure you would find in Disney's Hall of Presidents, this lackluster mute wordlessly nodded in the direction of several tubs of un-cancelled mail ten feet from where he was standing. We thanked him for his exertion, dropped the letter, and headed for home. Like clockwork, our orders were filled within the two-week time frame the agency had promised.

Knowing my kid sister Julie was a fan, I promised I'd take her along. She was understandably thrilled, it being her first concert and all. As of now, it was all systems go, T-minus twenty-four.

The next morning, even Boston's T commuter rail delay couldn't dampen my spirits. I busied my mind on the disabled train by giving careful consideration to all the possible hit songs the Stones would be performing from their vast catalogue of chart-busters.

After the train arrived at Park St. Station, I switched over to the T's green-line trolley and only had to ride it three-hundred yards before hopping off at Boylston Street. From there St. James was a mere five- minute walk.

I punched in and said my hellos, in a hurry to complete my first delivery rounds so I could rush up to Medical Transcriptions and pick Ginny's pretty little head to find out what songs the Stones had played the night before.

"Hey Ginny, how were they?" I blurted. "What was it like?"

"I never saw them," Ginny said. "They were busted at some airport in Rhode Island for assaulting a photographer, so Nick Sagger and I hung out till eleven-thirty and then went home. I did hear on the radio this morning that Mayor White had to pull some strings with the Warwick police chief to get them sprung. The mayor was able to persuade the chief to give them a police escort to the Boston Garden. I think they finally got on stage around 12:45 a.m." Ginny gave a defiant shake of her coiffed black tresses. "I wouldn't wait up that late to hear Pope Paul sing,"

"Would you still like to see them?" I absentmindedly inquired. "I've got tickets for tonight."

"Yeah, Tommy, I still want to see them!" she said in near disbelief. "I'll pay you face value for the ticket."

"I didn't want to sell it to you. I wanted to take you to it," I stammered. "Of course, I'll go with you tonight."

I told Ginny about the other couple who would be coming with us, got her phone number and address, and told her what time we would be by to get her.

The rest of the work day rushed by as if I were in some type of fragmented surreal dream.

On my way home, I realized I would have to break the news to Julie, that her older brother was now dashing her dreams by stiffing her out of a ticket.

The guilt associated with such a disturbing task left me less than a minute later, after I weighed the risk of Julie's heartbroken feelings versus the rewards for my own selfish desires. Besides, I reasoned, I could always placate Julie's trampled feelings the next time the Bay City Rollers came to town.

Once home, I called Buzzy. He told me they would swing by at 6:00 p.m. to pick me up. After Buzzy and Sudsy picked me up, we drove to the liquor store for a couple of G.I.Q.'s (giant imperial quarts of beer) before picking up Ginny.

In the interest of time, Buzzy said he'd jump out at the store to solicit a buyer, since the Mustang was a two-door, and I was in the back seat behind Sudsy. In less than five minutes, Buzzy collared a customer who was willing to buy us the beer, provided we would duke him a fin for his troubles. No sooner had our guy emerged from the store and turned over the beer order to Buzzy, when the Mets (Metropolitan Police) pulled up.

Sudsy and I watched as one of the cops grabbed the buyer while the other cop pushed Buzzy into the store wall. After checking the buyer's ID, the cop yelled at him and kicked him in the ass as he turned to leave. The cop who had nabbed Buzzy took one of the quart bottles out of the paper bag, unscrewed the cap and methodically drained the contents into Buzzy's pants pocket.

The Mustang was only six spaces over from the cruiser. Sudsy and I tried to sink into our seats so the cops wouldn't see us.

When the quart was empty, the cop gave Buzzy's pocket a hard slap either for emphasis or in homage to a bad Laurel and Hardy skit. They told Buzzy to screw before they changed their minds and ran him down to the station, but not before putting the other G.I.Q. in the back of their cruiser.

Seconds later Buzzy was getting behind the wheel. He smelled like the Haffenreffer Brewery. "Well kids, good news and bad news," he chirped.

"What's the good news?" I asked.

"They didn't lug me for underage drinking," he stated proudly.

"So, what's the bad news?"

"When they asked me my name, I gave them yours," he said sheepishly. Incredulous, I asked, "Why did you give them my name?"

"I don't know. I think I had a brain freeze."

"You didn't have it so bad that you knew enough to hang me instead of yourself," I protested.

"Oh, more bad news, too," he added. "That ounce of pot you had me buy for you got ruined, but you still owe me the twenty bucks for it."

"How did it get ruined?" I asked in disbelief.

Buzzy laughed. "It was in the same pocket the cop poured the beer into."

That's pissa! I thought. I was starting to feel the same type of benign revulsion for Buzzy that I would usually reserve for Jagger whenever I saw him start strumming an acoustic guitar on a stage stool, or Karen Carpenter settle in behind a drum kit with sticks in her hands.

Despite the police run-in, Buzzy and Sudsy's attitudes were so positive and upbeat that I soon found myself joking along with them about the whole episode. Buzzy swung by his house and changed his soaking, grungy jeans for a fresh pair, but inexplicably left on his smelly, Jethro Tull tee shirt.

By six-thirty, we had parked the car at a T parking lot and were on the green line trolley chugging down Commonwealth Avenue towards Ginny's apartment.

Ginny was outside waiting for us. After I made the introductions all around, we crossed the tracks we had just left, and walked to the opposite set of tracks that would take us to the Boston Garden. It was patently obvious from the enthusiasm, similar fashions, and same age of our fellow passengers that we were all headed to the same destination.

We pulled into North Station, disembarked and followed the crush of concert-goers into the Garden. Once in the vestibule of the Garden, the wave of humanity carried us past food vendors, ticket scalpers and seekers, and the ever-present homeless winos who milled about. Several vendor stands hawked ten-dollar Rolling Stones Tour tee shirts for thirty bucks. The entrepreneurial spirit of Woodstock was lost on no one.

Fifteen minutes later we were ensconced in our nosebleed seats, having climbed six stories of staircases to get there. The house lights went up in the old barn giving us a bird's eye view of the seventeen thousand celebrants, despite the building being blanketed in a haze of cigarette and marijuana smoke.

At 7:30 p.m., the lights went down and Stevie Wonder came out and performed an incredible set. Although I was present, I can neither confirm nor deny that Stevie allegedly ducked when some bozo tossed a tomato at him from the floor. Who brings tomatoes to a Stones concert?

Whether the crowd was antsy from the stories and rumors the Stones had generated the night before, or if they suffered from a collective, self-induced paranoia of their own making, I never knew. I did know that the forty-five-minute delay between acts only antagonized the crowd further.

At one point, nearly a half hour after Wonder's act was finished, about a dozen numbskulls on the floor tried to set their heavy wooden seats on fire. We watched dumbfounded from our mile-high seats. Luckily, for the remaining seventeen thousand fans, the Zippo lighters were no match for the twenty-five-pound folding chairs and wouldn't ignite. Fifteen minutes later, the five lads from the south of London, along with three black backup singers and a complete horn section, hit the stage.

The band opened with their electrifying take on *'Jumping Jack Flash.'* I glanced at Ginny when the band's second song, *'Bitch'* started and saw she was no longer beside me. I asked Buzzy and Sudsy where she went. They said she mentioned something about going down to the floor to see if the view was better.

I could feel my blood pressure rising from Ginny's absence with every Richard's riff. I hadn't been that upset since a mail order scheme had separated ten bucks from me, allegedly in return for a tee shirt with Brian Jones's sneering mug on it. When I wrote to the company about my missing shirt, I was informed that the post office box associated with the business had been closed.

Sometime between Jagger's fifth costume change and the band's rousing encore rendition of *'Satisfaction,'* Ginny had made her way back to our seats in tears.

"What's the matter, Ginny? Why, you seem…inconsolable," I said in the best, blasé monotone I could muster.

"I went down on the floor to see if I could get us better seats, and when I got there, I ran into Nick Sagger, and he was all over some pretty blonde," she spat between sobs.

"Oh, you mean you got jilted for another? That must suck," I muttered. "What! You don't believe me?" she cried. "Look down there, on the left side, about ten feet in front of Wyman's amps. He's wearing his scrubs and lab coat."

I looked down to where Ginny pointed. Sure enough, there was Nick Sagger, sashaying his skinny ass, like his alter ego on stage, to the final chords of the final song of the night. I must admit, Nick Sagger did appear to have that babe captivated by his charms, not unlike a spider to a fly. "That's him alright, but why did he wear his work togs to a concert," I asked in disbelief.

"He wears his scrubs for comfort and the jacket gives him an aura of authority," Ginny said.

"I suppose if Keith passes out on stage, and the band puts out a call for a doctor in the house, Nick Sagger could scramble up there and give him mouth-to-mouth."

Before Ginny could reply, the Stones had formed together center stage, took one prolonged bow, and disappeared into the blackness of the bowels of the Boston Garden.

The house lights came up, and the masses prepared to make the laborious trek down the mountain of stairs to the freedom of the summer night air.

Ginny turned in to me and asked if I could escort her home now. Despite the multitudes heading towards North Station, the T had wisely staggered their trolley schedule only a few minutes apart in order to quickly disperse the hoards.

We ended up standing near the end of our car, Buzzy and Sudsy talking softly, while Ginny and I engaged in awkward small talk. I suppose my conversation was too contrived for Ginny, because within minutes of boarding I watched as Ginny slowly backed away from me, shamelessly slinked into the crash of passengers, and once again disappeared out of my sight. I imagined she would excuse herself in work the next day by telling me she was merely getting ready to hop off at her stop, even though she still had another ten or eleven stops to go.

I started talking to Buzzy and Sudsy again. They didn't ask me about "Houdini's" whereabouts. When we reached Ginny's stop, I looked outside for her. I strained to see her moonlit figure at the exact instant she was struck, while trying to cross the tracks, head-on by the inbound trolley

The next day at work, everyone was buzzing about Ginny's accident. When Mrs. J. spotted me, she ushered me into her office to ask me about the events leading up to the accident. After I told her what I saw, she told me Ginny had been taken to St. James for treatment, was in a full body cast, but was expected to make a full recovery within several months.

After the initial excitement died down, I grabbed my overloaded delivery cart to begin my first clinic rounds. When I got to Medical Transcriptions, I noticed they had already filled Ginny's position with a pretty temp. Perhaps pretty is somewhat of an understatement. *Hottest frigging babe in the entire hospital* would be more like it.

I introduced myself. She told me her name was Olivia, and within minutes we were talking about our favorite rock bands.

"You know, Olivia, The Who are coming to Boston next month, and my friend Buzzy and I are going into the Garden next week to score some tickets, and well, I was just wondering…"

"Hey Mom, The Recliner Fell On Dad Again!"

Dad's thirty-fifth Memorial Mass came and went with the usual amount of fanfare one might expect for an earthly soul departed so long. Although many of my siblings and their spouses were in attendance; they made the mandatory beeline to the local beef-and-beer watering hole afterwards for the ritualistic "Celebration of Life" gathering.

I politely excused myself and headed home. Despite the lengthy passage of dad's demise, Celebration of Life was a euphemism I felt somewhat ambivalent about. Not that I was overly prudish. I just felt that sometimes the alcohol artificially fueled the celebration part, a hell of a lot more than the actual life part. On top of that, I was suffering from a never-ending man cold, and had I a ballot, would have unequivocally voted that doozy into the Ibuprofen Hall of Fame in its first year of eligibility.

Why, I don't suspect I was home more than ten minutes before an overpowering wave of sleepy time goodness enveloped my senses. My clothes fell to the floor in conspiratorial surrender to the will of my body and mind. I took the requisite ten-second count before in glorious victory, slumber raised its outstretched mitts over me.

I immediately fell into a REM state, and in somewhat of an outer body experience viewed my body, limbs perfectly splayed out at even intervals in relation to my torso. In the background large concentric rings slowly turned in a clockwise motion in precision with my centered form. I heard the heavenly strains of a celestial harp. Oh yeah, this was definitely a dream.

Seconds later, I found myself standing in my kitchen looking at my dad. He was seated at the table, noshing on a giant slab of Bundt cake that I had just finished icing before crashing.

He was decked out in his trademark porkpie hat and his favorite powder blue, polyester leisure suit, which he had croaked in. The only clothing oddity I could discern was, he wore golden slippers in place of his ever-present white "Superfly" loafers.

"Dad, what's up with the kicks? I've never seen you in slippers before." "It's a luxury I was allowed to take during my visit," he offered while shoveling fistfuls of cake into his pie-hole. "Plus, I feel like I'm walking on clouds in these bad boys."

"I always heard that the holy souls in heaven take the forms of fifteen-year-olds, and that whenever Jesus wishes to appear before his chosen ones, he would usually manifest himself in the guise of a teenager. So, Dad, why didn't you come back as some type of glorified Justin Beiber?"

"Because dumbass, you wouldn't have recognized me. Besides, I don't know who the hell this Justin dude is. You see, son, in heaven we aren't permitted to see all the comings and goings here on earth. God has put up a barrier larger than the Great Wall of China to obstruct our view. Sometimes though, when newbies pass through the gates, someone will pull them aside and pump them for dirt, before any of the angels spot them, of course."

"A structure larger than the Great Wall of China, Dad?" "Have I ever lied to you before son?"

"Seriously, Dad? You once told me I was born in a Japanese Internment Camp. Besides, how come God doesn't want you to see what's going on down here?" I pried.

"Because God doesn't want to bum us out. Perpetual bliss in paradise and misery on earth goes together like kittens and woodchippers. By the way, junior, when I was coming in for my landing, I noticed a car in your driveway with bald rear tires."

"That's impossible," I snorted. "That's my wife's new car, and she's still driving around on the same free tank of gas the dealership gave her two months ago. Any other observations, Dad?"

"Yeah, the state inspection sticker for your car parked out front has expired," he noted. "By the way, whatever happened to that '78 Dodge Scamp I sold you?"

"Geez Dad, that was over thirty-five years ago. It rusted from the inside out. The only things left were a crowbar, a tire jack and her slant-six engine. But boy, if that baby could talk."

"It'd bore me to tears?" dad deadpanned.

"Yo Pops, chill! You're going straight-up 'Timberlake Gangsta' on me now."

"Forget all that, son. Your mother, your poor sainted mother. How is she faring these days?"

"Pretty good, Dad. After you passed, she got remarried to a retired fertilizer salesman and moved to an over fifty-five village in Vegas. Hey, remember the time we went on that family vacation in New Hampshire, and you blew the entire bankroll at the dog track on our first day there? Mom's reaction was priceless!"

"Son, I hadn't seen a woman that furious since Helen Crump caught Andy flirting with that new blonde cashier at the Mayberry bakery."

"Say Pops, how about all those times your Lazy Boy fell on top of you?"

"Come on, son! Those were flukes. It only happened whenever I was racing to the window blinds before the Jehovahs could make it to our front door."

"Don't take this the wrong way, because I love seeing you," I said, "but were you sent here to show me what my future holds? Or maybe to inspire me to follow some sort of road to righteousness?"

"Hell no, kid!" he snorted. "I just felt like getting out. By the way, what's that little black gadget in your hand that you keep looking at?"

"It's called a cell phone," I said. "In addition to telephone calls, it can also give you the time, date, weather, breaking news and even Sudoku puzzles."

"Looks like a James Bond toy to me," dad chided. "That's exactly what it is, Pops."

"Son, what's the deal with all these people strutting around in their pajamas? I must've seen a half dozen of them when I was flying in."

"Casual is the new formal," I explained. "Savvy moms today proudly parade their musty misgivings to the beach, PTA meetings and even to houses of worship. As for the men, they've essentially transformed their Power Ranger pj's into the modern day business suit. They can hop a plane in their jammies, brainstorm around conference tables and be in lock step with their flannel-minded brethren. After networking and decompressing back at the hotel lounge, they can snuggle in their beds, already clad in their nighties."

"Huxley was right, son. It is a brave new world. When I was a Young Turk, whores dressed like ladies, and ladies dressed like whores. Any self-respecting woman wouldn't be caught dead taking out the garbage without first putting her hair up and make-up on. A dinner date would get you an Audrey Hepburn look-a-like, complete with pearl necklace, elbow-high white gloves, and nylons with those devilish seams. Damn! Those seams were like flashing neon arrows, directing our unsuspecting glances over shapely calves until they cruelly disappeared beneath a perfectly-tailored herringbone skirt, letting our unspeakable desires run unfettered and unforgiven."

"Dad, you forgot unfulfilled!" I paused, and asked, "Pops, after a person dies, how long does it take before they find out where they're going for eternity?"

"The Almighty renders a judgment and final placement of one's disposition in the time it takes a bald man to dry his hair after emerging from the sea."

"Are you speaking in parables?"

"Verily, I say to you, ye shall be judged in the same amount of time it takes a hungry man to eat his dinner."

"Okay, Dad. I get it!"

"Tell me, kid, what's the biggest change in the world since I've been gone?"

"Technology," I stated. "The Internet has probably had the most profound effect on mankind. Communication and news around the planet is nearly instantaneous. That's put the print media nearly back in the Stone Age, because now everyone has information at their fingertips. The human toll on all this has resulted in more isolation and alienation. I guess you could say, civility went out the window not long after *The Adventures of Ozzie and Harriet* went off the air."

"By the way son, what do you do for work?" dad asked. "I remember for years you had some crazy notion of becoming either a stage coach driver or a sheep herder."

"Yeah, those jobs really didn't pan out. My dream job was to be a monorail operator at Disney World. They give their drivers these cool blue and yellow uniforms, plus the ten percent company discount to all the parks and shops, including the Bibboty Bobbity Liquor Store."

"No wonder it's the Happiest Place on Earth," dad stated.

"When they sent me the rejection letter for being under-qualified, I hooked up with Sears. I've bounced around in a half-dozen departments in the twenty-odd years I've been there. Right now, I'm in Home Goods, selling vacuum cleaners, but lately, employee morale has been at an all-time low."

"In heaven's name, son, why?"

"A few months ago, a new hire in Sporting Goods was caught on video swiping just about everything that wasn't nailed down. The final straw was when he was spotted boosting a neon orange kayak on his head. Luckily, the cameras got a positive make on him by his signature black socks and sandals. The store manager interviewed him, he confessed and was summarily dismissed for grand larceny.

"A few months later, the ex-employee hired a lawyer who got his case before an arbitrator. The arbitrator had one question for the manager: "Did you, at any time, inform the employee that stealing was wrong, against store policy, and was not a requirement of his position?"

"Not a requirement of his position? Why no…of course not," the manager stammered.

The arbitrator reproached the manager, declaring: "This court finds in favor of the plaintiff. The Sears Holding Company shall re-instate the aggrieved to his former position forthwith, shall make full restitution in lost wages, sick leave, and vacation time so that the claimant is made whole. Said company shall also incur all costs pursuant to this hearing. Case closed."

"Jeez, that's a tough pill, son," dad said, "but look on the good side—you're still gainfully employed, and Sears always did have a great employee profit-sharing plan."

"All true, Dad, but the other shoe dropping is Amazon." "The river or the jungle son?"

"Neither! You see, Pops, Amazon is an online conglomerate that can fill and ship every product from A to Z, and deliver your dinner while you're waiting. Many people today are shopping exclusively online, thereby putting malls and mom and pop stores out of business."

"Nonsense!" dad exclaimed. "America will always need Craftsmen tools and Kenmore washers and dryers."

"Amazon sells those too, Dad."

"Son, I think my little earthly excursion has been an eye-opener for the both of us, but I really have to be getting back now. They're showing a Marx Brothers double-feature tonight, and if you come in late, they make you clean the popcorn machine afterwards. I'll be seeing you around son, and don't forget that your car's state inspection sticker has…expired."

"Seeing me around?... expired? Parables again, Dad? Are you trying to tell me something Dad?…DAD?…DAAAAD?"

Silent Cal, The Big Train & The '24 Senators

I, Jimmy Hatchet, do solemnly attest, to the best of my recollection and knowledge, that the facts hereby written within these pages are accurate, complete and true, as to their stated veracity, on this eight-day of December, nineteen-hundred and seventy-four, in the year of our Lord.

"Hatchet, get in here!" I heard my editor, Cy Sweeney barking my name out for the third time that morning. The first time was for his coffee and Danish, the second was to run copy to the advertising department, and this was for only-God-knows-what. I entered his office with more anxiety than normal due to the extra urgency in his voice.

"Yes, Mr. Sweeney?" I answered in anticipation. "You wanted to see me?"

"Hatchet, Dotson is out today, so you're going to have to cover the White House for us this afternoon," he commanded. "The president is giving a statement on balancing the budget, and I need you there for coverage."

"But Mr. Sweeney, I'm not a political writer, I'm a sports reporter," I protested.

"I don't care if you're Grantland Rice. Today you're covering the president's press release. Besides, all you have to do is take notes and keep your yap shut. The president hates these things as much as we do, and he'll wrap it up in no time flat," he snapped.

There I was, not quite two years out of Georgetown as a journalism major, toiling on the lowest rung under the auspices of the Washington Herald Sports Department.

Only today, I was entrusted with morphing into H.L. Mencken, turning in similar mesmerizing political prose as I envisioned the acclaimed Baltimorean would do. I took a quick mental inventory of my lot, both socially and career-wise and surmised that at twenty-five, the good far outweighed the bad, despite my non-existent social life concerning the fairer sex.

Despite my total social blackout and my tenuous position regarding my cantankerous editor, the summer of '24 in the District of Columbia had one unmistakable thing going for it: Walter Johnson and the Washington Senators. The Nationals had risen from a fourth place finish the previous year to eek out the pesky Tigers and the dreaded Yankees, staking their first pennant in team history. Beating out the detested Gothams with the boorish Babe Ruth by a mere two games was the ice cream on the pie.

Washington couldn't get enough of their beloved Senators and especially Walter Johnson, 'The Big Train' himself. About the only baseball honor the thirty-six-year-old, flame-throwing pitcher didn't possess was a World Series title. Along with player-manager Bucky Harris, Goose Goslin, Sam Rice and a swarm of too many others to mention, I would be in no small measure, tasked with faithfully reporting on the team's successes and God forbid, failures against the invincible John McGraw and his mighty New York Giants for baseball's ultimate prize.

For the present, I would have to content myself with going to the White House and recording every utterance I could jot down from the 30th President of the United States, Calvin Coolidge.

The Herald was several blocks away from the White House, but with the weather being what it was for late September, I decided to hoof it over. This being my first visit inside 1600 Pennsylvania Avenue, I hadn't the foggiest notion where the press corps assembled, but when I got there, a doorman was gracious enough to give me precise directions to the assigned room.

When I entered the designated area, I was surprised to see such a small gathering of my colleagues. Perhaps only a half dozen, talking amongst themselves and setting up their photography equipment. I quietly slid to the back of the scrum, and because I knew nary a soul, felt unencumbered to make small talk with the lot of them. I soon found myself distracted, looking up at the large oil portraits of statesmen on the wall, none of whom I recognized.

Moments later, a man, whose only distinguishable features were that he had none, entered the room by himself and walked over to the podium to address us. With a nod in our direction, and absent any pleasantries exchanged to those he may have known, the President began to spill out a barrage of numbers, dates and trends that came out of his mouth like a flash flood of alphabet soup.

Luckily for me, the President paused long enough to illustrate his figures and projections by putting large graphs printed on poster boards onto a tripod beside the lectern.

This visual aid served the dual purpose of allowing us enough time to copy the pertinent information, along with actually being able to follow and understand what the President was saying. When the President completed his discourse after five minutes, he allowed the press three questions, because as he stated, "I hate repeating myself." He answered the questions, thanked us for coming, and disappeared down a long hallway.

I spent another five minutes in the room, double-checking that all the info I had copied was indeed accurate, before heading out.

I had put my pad and pencil away and, being preoccupied with what had just transpired, I inadvertently took a wrong turn on my way out to find the exit.

Nervously, I began to work my way down the cavernous corridor, checking every closed door I came upon. I walked into one and quickly realized I had entered the White House kitchen.

Before I could turn to rectify my mistake, I heard a voice call out to me, "Hey *Herald*, come 'ere."

I turned to see Calvin Coolidge sitting on a pickle barrel, eating blueberry pie and waving me over.

"I'm sorry to disturb you, Mr. President. I got lost. I don't know what I was thinking," I coughed up.

"You were thinking you found the right door," the President shot back.

The President looked more relaxed in this setting, whereas in the press room he had carried a dour expression not unlike one who had just consumed a bushel of lemons. If nothing else, the blueberry stains ringing his mouth did serve to soften his cranky disposition.

"What's your name, kid and where are you from?" the President demanded.

"Hatchet, sir. Jimmy Hatchet and I'm from Boston. Came down here to attend G-town and after I graduated, got a job at the *Herald* as a sports reporter."

"Looks like now we're a couple of transplanted Red Sox fans, rooting for our adopted Senators," the former Governor of Massachusetts stated.

"Yes sir, Mr. President, but it sure was fun watching 'Smokey Joe' Wood, Tris Speaker and 'the Babe' win all those titles," I said.

"Call me, Cal, Jimmy. I agree. It was a hoot watching those fellas play, although I always felt Ruth had a million-dollar arm and a ten-cent brain. Course, it's pretty hard to argue with the success Walter Johnson's had, this season or any other."

At this juncture a beefy-looking bureaucrat entered the kitchen, scanned his surroundings, approached the President, and asked him for his signature on several documents. He glanced at me with a hint of annoyance as the President obliged him and handed them back without saying a word. The functionary thanked the president, and left the kitchen.

"Who was that, Cal?" I asked.

"Herbert Hoover, my Secretary of Commerce. He means well, but he's always giving me advice…unsolicited, I might add. Mark my words. If that fella ever comes into real power, this country will be in the outhouse, lickety split."

Cal wolfed down a hunk of peach cobbler and started to get a little sentimental while reminiscing about one of the legendary pitchers of his youth, "Pud" Galvin. "Say what you will about these modern athletes today, but I don't see any of them reeling off ninety-two wins over two seasons like Ol Pud did for the Buffalo Bison's back in '83-84. Why, he was so effective, he once threw a six-hit, three-two victory over the Cincinnati Red Stockings," Cal claimed.

"What's so impressive about that?" I snorted.

"Because Pud pitched the entire game from second base," Cal cackled. "Pud did fancy himself quite the Jim Dandy among the women-folk, especially between innings. Who knows how many more games he would have won absent those small indiscretions?"

"Ninety-two wins over a two-year stretch is a crazy crooked number, Cal, but did you ever hear that The Big Train once blanked the Yanks three times in a four-day span early in his career? And he improved with each subsequent outing, tossing six-, four- and two-hitters. Heck, using that logic, doesn't it stand to reason that he was on pace to no-hit them had he faced them once more?" I argued.

"You don't have to sell me on that big galoot. I'm all on board the Johnson Express," Cal assured me. "Course, the poetry of it all is how Walter incorporates his shoulder, arm, and hand movements with the same precision-like motion of a calibrated piston in a Model-T."

"You certainly won't get any argument from some of the best hitters in the game like Cobb, Hornsby or Traynor." I seconded. "They'll tell you to a man that Johnson is the quickest in the game, bar none. Ty's even stated on record, that with Walter's windmill wind-up and monkeyish long arms, a batter can practically reach out and shake hands with him from the box. And old Tyrus should know. He's been battling Johnson since Walter came up in '07."

"Yep," Cal agreed. "Johnson was just blessed with more horsepower in that right arm than anybody else who toes the rubber."

I thanked the President for his time, realizing that I had spent over an hour at the White House and had to file my report in order to make the afternoon edition.

When I checked back to my paper, one of the office copy boys told me Sweeney had been looking for me. I gave my report to a business editor and headed towards Sweeney's office. When I got there, Sweeney was in an uncharacteristically cheery mood and told me to take a seat.

"Hatchet, I just got off the horn with Coolidge, and it seems you hit it off pretty good with him. He wants you to cover the house for all his pronouncements."

"But, Mr. Sweeney, I don't know politics," I pleaded.

"You don't know sports either, but you still got a job, right?" Sweeney laughed. "Anyways, don't worry about covering politics. Dobson is back here on Monday. The president said he liked you because you didn't ask any questions. He does have another task for you, though. He wants you to cover all the away games at the Polo Grounds when the series commences. There is a catch, though. The President wants you to record the games using a scorecard and then relay the info to the White House from a telegraph office after each game. Mr. Coolidge wants to be the first one in D.C. to get the results."

"This is the first time you're sending me to cover road games, Mr. Sweeney," I said. "When will I be leaving, and where will I be staying while I'm in New York for the three games there?"

"You'll be leaving for New York next week on October 5th, and returning on the eighth," he said. "If the series goes that far and the Pullman doesn't break down, you should make it back to Griffith Stadium in time for Game 6. You can see my secretary Adele, on your way out the door. She'll give you the train tickets, press credentials and directions to the boarding house you'll be staying at."

"Boarding house?" I shrieked. "I thought all the reporters on assignment stayed in hotels!"

"That's only for our senior correspondents," Sweeney explained. "You bush leaguers will be breaking bread with the common man for the foreseeable future. One more thing, Hatchet. The Senators are holding their last, light workout today at Griffith before the series starts in a few days. Go down there and see if you get any newsworthy quotes, especially from Johnson. Every paper in town is going to be covering this, so it'll be a free-for-all," Sweeney warned.

"Why would Walter Johnson give any quotes to a bush leaguer?" I asked.

"Because," Sweeney shot back, pointing at me, "this bush leaguer personally knows the President of the United States, and so does he."

When I arrived at the stadium, the Senators had just completed their workout and were coming off the field and heading towards the showers. I headed down a corridor towards the locker room with about thirty other reporters, getting shoved and jostled like everyone else. We waited twenty minutes at the locker room door before player-manager Bucky Harris came out and gave us the rundown.

"Okay boys, okay…. settle down. Tell you what. You can have fifteen minutes with them and then everybody out. It was sumbitch of a season for us. Some of the fellas are nicked up a bit and some just need a breather. I'm giving them off tomorrow and then Game 1 starts the following day. So, come on in, get ya quotes and then beat it!" Bucky instructed.

It was one of the things that everyone who covered the team liked about Bucky. He was a straight shooter who always gave it to you on the square. He could flash leather at second base and was a crackerjack at turning the double play. Naturally, when the door opened, about thirty reporters tried to squeeze through it at the same time.

Luckily for me, the crush carried me right to the front of Johnson's locker. Walter had just finished showering and dressing. As he combed his hair, he shouted, "Okay boys, fire away!"

For several minutes I was drowned out by a half dozen reporters all shouting questions. I waited for a lull and then shamelessly played my presidential card. "Mr. Johnson, the President says to say 'hello and good luck' in Game 1," I blurted. The clubhouse fell deathly quiet and I felt the eye of every soul present squarely on me. The Big Train turned in my direction and asked, "You know Mr. Coolidge?"

"Why yes, of course," I answered with as much conviction as I could feign.

"So do I," Johnson replied. "Tell you a funny one, bush. Two years ago, Mr. Coolidge invited me to Northampton, Massachusetts for some grouse hunting near his farm. Well, to hear ol' Cal tell it, he was quite the crack shot as a young buck and at one point, fancied himself the finest shooter growing-up in Vermont. On this day, Cal had me march some three miles in the woods before he stops to rest a spell, and to take care of some urgent business behind a large spruce. He no sooner returns to me and damn, if he doesn't spot a twenty-five-pound Tom preening like a peacock on a log, not twenty paces from where we were situated.

"Cal silently raises his twelve-gauge, takes aim, fires…and misses, as the turkey flies off. Well sir, that set me off on a fit of laughter not unlike that of a lunatic. The more I laughed, the madder Cal got. The madder Cal got, the harder I laughed. It was a terrible cycle I must confess. I hadn't the nerve to tell Cal that I had swapped out his birdshot for blank caps while he was behind the tree, until both our weapons were unloaded and safely stored away for the day.

"Joking aside, kid," continued Johnson, "I wouldn't mess about Cal if I didn't love him. Today, young ladies are busy flapping, men are drinking bathtub gin and devil-dogs are walking on the wings of aeroplanes. Mr. Coolidge has the comportment and a sense of propriety to dedicate his duties looking out for the welfare of the country. While some aren't content if they're not in the spotlight or making complete fools of themselves, Cal is keeping his eye on the ball, cutting taxes, chopping out needless bureaucracies and reducing the deficit. I'm sorry, kid, I didn't mean to climb on my soapbox, spouting off needlessly. Did you have a baseball question for me?" Johnson inquired.

"Just one, Mr. Johnson," I said. "The Giants have won the series two out of the past three years. How ya fixing to pitch to their sluggers, Hack Wilson and High Pockets Kelly in Game 1?"

"High heat, kid. High heat," Walter drawled.

I got some more quotes from Bucky and their scrappy shortstop, Roger Peckinpaugh before I headed back to the office to file my story. On my way back to the *Herald*, I noticed how the whole town seemed to have an extra spring in its step. The towns' rival papers and other news outlets couldn't get enough of the Nats, especially old Walt. It seems the entire town's confidence was predicated on the success of Johnson's mighty windmill motion and his sidewinder delivery.

My mind starting to spin on the notion that I had met and seen the two biggest attractions in D.C. since the Lincoln Memorial and Washington Monument went up. Taking stock of my newfound acquaintances, I realized that neither Cal nor Walter smoked, drank nor chewed. They both were principled men who eschewed adulation and preferred the humble solitude of their own company.

Cal was as economical with the spoken word as Walter was with the effortless manner in which he heaved the horsehide. Two diverse occupations as one could find, with relatively the same outcome: unmitigated success in their respective fields.

On Saturday, October 4th, the combatants from both clubs locked into an epic twelve-inning match that saw the heavily-favored Giants squeeze out a 4-3 win. Both hurlers, Art Neff and Walter Johnson went the distance, but New York prevailed when they scored two runs in the final frame while the Nats could only manage one in their half, stranding a man on third.

The following day, Washington knotted the series up, one-all, with the identical score from the previous day, 4-3.

Bucky and Goose Goslin sparked the offense, each socking solo home runs.

The next three games would be played away at the Polo Grounds and, thanks to Coolidge, I would be making my first road series for the *Herald*.

Armed with my official Major League Baseball scorecards, I dutifully recorded Game 3 in a dreadfully mundane contest, scoring it 6-4, in favor of the Giants. About the only excitement came in the bottom of the seventh, when Giant's manager John McGraw surreptitiously had about a dozen wheelchairs pushed out to the outfield foul lines between innings. The plan was ostensibly to interfere with any balls hit in that vicinity to trip up the Washington outfielders. McGraw's chicanery was as diabolical as it was genius. The wily manager employed the use of white uniforms for his faux orderlies as well as W.W. I army fatigues for those who would be posing as his invalids. As soon as the Giants were out at the bottom of their inning, the wheelchairs would magically disappear from foul ground territory.

When the Senators took the field in the eighth and the wheelchairs re-appeared, Harris noticed the ploy and quickly brought it to umpire Bill Klem's attention. Klem glared at McGraw before shouting, "GET THOSE CRIPPLES OUTTA THERE!" Klem bellowed so loud that the fakers in the wheelchairs stood up and high-tailed it out of there before their phony attendants had a chance to push them away.

Those in attendance, knowing what McGraw was capable of in order to gain the slightest edge over an opponent, showered the entire park in gales of laughter, mixed with hoots of derision towards Klem.

At the game's conclusion, I ran to the nearest telegraph office outside the park and paid the clerk an extra dollar for the additional time and effort he would expend to get my scorecard results wired to Washington.

Back at Mrs. Willouby's boarding house, where I was staying, I foolishly made the mistake of telling the other boarders my occupation. As it was, I only had to eat crow one night in front of my supper guests, after the Game 3 loss. The dinner table was uncharacteristically quiet after Washington won Game 4, 7-4.

I hopped back on the Pullman immediately after I telegraphed D.C. with the Senator's Game 5 loss, 6-2. Sadly, this was Johnson's second series loss in as many outings, and whether it was due to dead arm following his Game 1 twelve-inning heartbreaker, or just the sign of an aging hurler whose arm had finally struck midnight, I never knew. I just knew, as my car pulled out of Grand Central Station, that if the baseball gods were to smile on the Senators in '24, the Nats would have to take two at home, with or without The Big Train.

Game 6 brought the nation's capital to its undivided attention. With the season riding on the line, Washington sent its other ace, Tom Zachary to the hill to square off against Game 1 victor, Art Nehf. After allowing one run in the first to the Giants, Zachary shut out the New Yorkers the following eight innings to square the series 3-all.

October 10th was Game 7, and the city was bursting with anticipation and anxiety in equal distribution. Why, it seemed completely possible that the city's youngest citizens, as well as its most feeble-minded, were all aware of the excitement and the stakes riding on the city's hopes that day. Using all the guile normally possessed by his counterpart across the diamond, Bucky outfoxed the great and venerable John McGraw himself. Harris duped McGraw by starting right-hand pitcher Curly Ogden for the first two batters of the game. He then handed the ball over to his stellar lefty, George Mogridge, boxing McGraw in with an all right-handed line- up.

Mogridge took the Nats into the eighth trailing 3-1, when Harris hit a two-run "bad hop" single over third baseman's Fred Lindstrom's head to tie it up.

In the ninth, Harris goes to Johnson telling him, "You're the best we got, Walter. We win or lose with you."

Inspired? Invigorated? Call it what you will. The Big Train throws four scoreless innings as the Senators swipe the deciding victory in the twelfth inning. This time, it's Earl McNeely hitting another "bad hop" single over the hapless Freddy Lindstrom's head, scoring Muddy Ruel from second.

Washington's long drought in baseball's equivalent to purgatory was finally over. The city erupted into a spontaneous celebration that seemed to combine Christmas, New Years and the 4th of July into one giant orgy of happiness and relief that carried on into the early morning hours.

It took weeks before the city came back down to earth and regained any semblance of normalcy in its day-to-day operations. The last images I had of Cal and Walter on that historic day were of the president in his box, tears in his eyes, grinning ear-to-ear and watching, as Johnson's teammates hoisted him out of the dugout, onto their shoulders, and carried him around his mound one more time in glorious victory.

Epilogue

Three years after the Washington Senators won the World Series, my personal life was to change in no small way. In December of '27, I applied for and accepted a position from my hometown newspaper, the *Boston Record* as a beat writer for the Red Sox. Aside from a promising sports career, I would also be back home with family and friends.

For his part Coolidge did what he did best. He propagated the concept that the "business of America was business," and acted accordingly. He reduced taxes so that at one point in his administration, only the top two percent of the population were paying taxes. In addition, he reduced the national debt by twenty-five percent between 1923-1929. Weary and content with a job well done, Cal decided against running for a second term, retiring to his Northampton farm in '29.

Walter Johnson pitched for a few more seasons before hanging them up for good at the conclusion of the '27 season. He came back to manage the Senators and the Cleveland Indians from '29 thru '35.

On February 22, 1936, a forty-eight year old Johnson was coaxed out of retirement to replicate the legend of George Washington throwing a silver dollar across the Rappahannock River, in honor of the presidents 204th birthday.

The townsfolk of Fredericksburg, Virginia, who were sponsoring the stunt, came out on both sides of the river to cheer on the old baseball warhorse one final time. Armed with three silver coins,

Johnson reared back and fired off the first practice one, which sank in the river. Putting extra mustard on his second warm-up toss, the coin made it to the opposite bank to the crowds unbridled delight. On Walter's final "official" toss, he put enough juice on the coin to fly fourteen feet over the 362 foot expanse, victorious once again.

For all Walter's wins, strikeouts and his incredible string of 110 shutouts, perhaps his greatest asset wasn't the possession of his right arm so much as his right character and disposition.

As for me, I eventually married, raised a family and worked my way up at the *Record* from beat reporter to Columnist to Managing Sports Editor over a forty-year career. Unbeknownst to me, the '24 Senators would be the last hometown winning championship team I would ever cover. Although the Red Sox came close, they came up a buck short and a day late to the '46 and '67 Cardinals, losing both Game 7's in heartbreaking fashion.

In hindsight, I suppose my career could have been a lot worse. I could have been covering the Cubs for all those years.

As for the Senators? Well, although they won the pennant the following year, and again in '33, they were for the most part, regulated to dwell in the dustbin of the American League cellar till this day. In a sense, it made the '24 season that much more sweeter, because for one fleeting moment in that late Indian summer sun, that "Washington Nine"—made up of a plucky manager, a squad of overachieving underdogs, and an aging pitcher too proud to give in to the ravages of time—were world champions forever.

INTERMISSION

Dance Of The Deacon

Part 1

"Get le scarpe! Get le scarpe!" the old woman cried in her half-English, half-Italian dialect.

"Vito, what is your nana saying?" I asked.

"She's telling me to get her shoes, and I have to find them before I can go out," he said.

I was standing in the second-floor back hallway of Vito Zito's house, impatiently waiting the sixty seconds it took for Vito to find and give his grandmother the heavy, black, clunky shoes that all women her age wore in 1962.

Mission accomplished.

We said our goodbyes to Vito's nana, raced down the back stairs and stepped outside where my older brother Jackie was waiting.

Jackie was the oldest sibling in my household, and outranking me by a year and a half, so he never wasted an opportunity to take advantage of me whenever the situation presented itself. That included me being the one who always called for our mutual friends while he stayed outside. It was an unwritten rule that stood in time memoriam. Ten-year-olds generally tended to do the bidding of their older brothers, no matter how mundane or unsavory the task may be. And Jackie was no exception. He exercised and abused this code as long as I would allow it, which I believe ended around the time I was thirteen.

I was the second oldest, christened Thomas J. McCauley and duly baptized in the one, holy, Catholic and apostolic church. Both my parents were first generation babies born in Boston of Irish stock on both sides, although dad's mother did claim a quarter cup of Scottish ancestry. Being Depression babies, mom and dad were baptized under the yoke of labor, confirmed in the spirit of accountability, and married in a state of shared sacrifice. To keep them honest, they were graced with the eighth sacrament of good old-fashioned Catholic guilt. To hear them tell it, they weren't satisfying all the tenants of the faith if they weren't in a perpetual state of some form of suffering.

Like the rest of their generation, their lives were fortified with all the character traits necessary to tackle any hardships World War II would throw their way. A few years after the war, dad was discharged from the Marines, met and married mom, and settled down to raise a family. Unfortunately, being reared between the twin crucibles of the Depression and a world war was no guarantee that raising six kids was going to be a cakewalk.

By the summer of '62, the family was complete. On this first day of July, my only concern was watching the weekly neighborhood touch football game. The game acquired its newfound popularity with the rising emergence of the NFL—along with the Kennedy's version of how the game was to be played—on the lawns of Hyannis Port. About the only thing that could ruin that game was if an errant pass landed in Mr. Fennessey's front yard while he was home.

Mr. Fennessey was the neighborhood grouch who wouldn't give you your ball back. Word had it that he had a plate in his head, received in battle while serving as an armored tank commander, which had changed his personality. Being only six or seven when I first heard about his condition, I assumed it was the type of plate you would use to set the dining room table with. I reasoned it was also why Mr. Fennessey called all the kids on the street "Jimmy," even the girls.

These contests were staged on my street with my front yard serving as the fifty-yard line. Shit, this vantage point was better than the grandstand reserve at Fenway. My yard was elevated four feet above the sidewalk, or in this case, the sidelines. We also had a three-foot chain-link fence that we used for slouching on. Depending on the accuracy of that day's QB, the fence also served as protection from errant throws—intentional or otherwise. The rules for the game were pretty straightforward: The distance between two telephone poles served as the goalposts, sidewalks were out of bounds, and flying colors didn't count.

The only variance from the rules were that forward passes were allowable, and each team got three downs instead of four to move the chains. The chains were an imaginary visual agreed upon by both teams that at least some yardage had been gained on the previous play. These scrums were staged between the block's big bananas, kids roughly aged thirteen to sixteen. The only exception was that if one side was short a player, they might grudgingly let one of us small fry engage. Some of the combatants were sandlot legends. First, there was Charlie and Mary Harney, siblings who almost always teamed together.

The street had it that Big Charlie could wing a pigskin the length of thirteen telephone poles. Although no video exists today, it was generally accepted as gospel back then. Big Charlie's sister Mary was as athletic and ornery as nearly every other player on the field.

Then there was the infamous Kevin Cullen—patron saint of bullies far and wide, who, when he wasn't washing our faces out with snow in the winter, was making us kiss his farts in the summer; and Kevin was one of the classier bullies. More importantly, he had good hands.

The last of the notables was Buddy Hill. Buddy's feats of athletic prowess and daredevil exploits were beyond the pale. Rumor had it that it was Buddy who had stolen the giant black boots off the Santa Claus display on top of Mal's department store the previous

Christmas. Handsome, athletic, and with a devil-may-care attitude to spare. Hell, we even thought Lloyd Price was singing about Buddy when we heard his hit single, *'Personality'* on our transistors. Buddy possessed all the confidence and swagger of Arnie Palmer putting a charge on the back nine at Cherry Hills in '60, swiping the Open from some rookie named Nicklaus. Buddy Hill had it all.

The rest of the players were basically the local backbenchers needed to round out the sides, five on five. Big Charlie and Mary anchored one team, while Buddy and Kevin were the studs on the other. Jackie, Vito, and I took our positions and settled in as the score went back and forth until the match was tied up, nine-all. The next touchdown would win.

Since Team Harney had just scored to knot up the game, both teams lined up at their opposite goals and waited for Big Charlie to pass off.

Buddy was playing deep, about twenty feet in the back of the end zone. Charlie reared back and let fly a perfect spiral five feet over Buddy's head. Buddy scrambled back, caught the pass on the fly and barely got the ball out of the end zone, before getting tagged.

As his team's QB, Buddy quickly marched the team up field with a series of buttonhooks, down-and-outs and stop-and-go's to Kevin. Buddy and Kevin were clicking like the second coming of Johnny U. and Ray Berry in the '58 championship game. Then it was third down, thirty feet from the end zone. Everyone was thinking a Hail Mary. Buddy took the snap, sent three-deep including Kevin, and held one decoy back near the line of scrimmage.

The entire defense went deep with Kevin except for the counter. Buddy faked the bomb, and before the counter could say, "three Mississippi" Buddy swerved left, dodged around him and headed upfield on a draw play. When the defense saw it was a run, two came in and two stayed back with Kevin. Buddy used his decoy to block, and when the defenders got too close, he pushed the decoy into them, taking all three out of the play.

With ten feet separating Buddy from the goal line, one more defender rushed in to put the drive-ending tag on him. Buddy tossed the ball to himself four feet into the air, at the same exact time the tag was applied. The ball dropped back into his arms, he cradled it, and stepped into the end zone. Game, set and match! It was the oldest trick in the schoolyard playbook, and despite the obvious chicanery, it was all perfectly legit.

Buddy Hill would never live to see his twentieth birthday. He was shot and killed in November of '66 when, during a recon mission in some godforsaken jungle in Vietnam, he walked with his platoon into an ambush. Wasn't that the way it always is with legends? Sampson? Caesar? Jesse James? Either ambushed, betrayed, or both?

At the end of the game, most of the older kids split up and went their separate ways, ceding the street back to us younger kids. Initially, Vito was going to run home and swipe his dad's magnifying glass so that we could fry ants on the sidewalk. When we saw the Cosgrove twins headed our way, we decided instead that we would have enough guys to get in several games of "King" before suppertime.

The Cosgrove twins, Billy and Hank, were a few years older than me. King usually had four or five players, and the object of the game was simple. The players would spread out on the street, throwing an Indian rubber ball against a wall. The rebound had to be caught cleanly by the player that the ball came closest to. You were awarded a letter for every time you either muffed the catch, or it got by you, until you had the four letters spelling out K-I-N-G. The loser would stand facing the wall and the rest of the players got to take three potshots apiece at him.

Since everyone was keeping score, it was customary to start "working on" the first player who was up to the letter N. When you did reach N, all bets were off. You'd have thought it was feeding time at the Franklin Park Zoo.

Everyone went into overdrive. The balls started coming one-way: Yours! In addition to running right up to the wall to put extra mustard on the ball, they also weren't above throwing screens at you a split second before the ball got to you.

Other than that, the game was pretty much on the square. Any way you cut it, when you lost you always ended up with a sore, red ass because the guys were always aiming for your nuts. Go figure, right? Most times, in their over zealousness to maul your balls, their shots would inevitably go wild. Served them right. Mind you, this was at close range.

After five or six games, we all saw Mr. Cosgrove heading towards us to get Billy and Hank for supper. Talk about being saved by the bell. The twins were the only ones at N when the game ended. I had lost two games myself, and neither twin had shown me any quarter when I was on the firing line. I did get a small measure of satisfaction when Mr. Cosgrove stuck his meaty fingers halfway down Hank's throat to mine-sweep free a giant wad of Bazooka bubble gum. He wasn't gentle about it, either.

Hank had swiped the gum when Vito was up against the wall and didn't notice it when the pack dropped out of his chinos. Cripes, Hank must have jammed five pieces into his trap before Vito got wise. You could tell when his dad took it out of his mouth that Hank hadn't had time to chew or suck half the sugar out of it. Truth be known, I thought Mr. Cosgrove was there to confront Billy about the carton of cigarettes he had found in the bushes of their driveway the day before. I'm sure Mr. Cosgrove knew Billy had stolen them from the supermarket, but what he didn't realize was that Billy had already stolen them back from him. One-zip, Billy!

As Jackie and I went into our house, we said "hello" to dad who was watching the Sox in the living room. It must have been a Yankees game, because dad unconsciously grunted back to us. Mom was starting to get supper going, and I could tell she wasn't having her best day. My four younger siblings were already in the kitchen and starting to turn up the volume. My baby sister, Patty was in her high chair, getting more of the Spaghetti-O's in her hair than in her mouth. The six-year-old twins were fighting because Barry was "looking at Bobby," while four-year-old Mikey was singing some song that had no rhyme or reason to it.

Saturday evening was hot-dogs-and-beans night, and to me that meant the living was easy. It didn't make it easier for dad, though.

The ice cream guy had just parked his truck in front of the house and left the nonstop nursery rhyme jingle blaring from his loudspeakers. As soon as the kids started yelling for ice cream, mom started to lose it.

Dad raced to the screen door and hollered at the ice cream guy to, "Get your shit box away from my house, now!"

After the ice cream guy said something about it being a public street, dad told him to, "Go shit in his hat," even though he wasn't wearing one.

After giving dad the stink eye for a moment, the ice cream guy thought better of it when he saw dad walk out onto the porch. He closed his little serving window, and went to move his truck … two houses down.

By this time, mom had Patty out of her chair and was washing her up and putting her in pajamas. After mom had the baby settled, we heard dogs crying and howling outside our door. Some were milling around on our porch while others took their positions on the front steps.

Duchess, our Border Collie mix, was in heat, and this "mating ritual" was starting to become a daily occurrence.

Well, that finally tore it for dad. He marched into the kitchen and grabbed the can of beans off the counter and headed towards the porch. Dad swung open the door and the half dozen dogs assembled scattered down the stairs. The last one down the stairs was a large black mongrel. I don't know if he was the last to leave because he was the alpha or because he was the horniest. Didn't matter. Dad reared back and brought heat—high and tight, professor. Dad's perfect strike combined the unmistakable intent of a Drysdale beanball with the searing velocity of a Koufax fastball, sending that mutt scurrying off with one aching arse.

You'd have thought that by dad putting out another fire, peace would have reigned supreme over Happy Valley. Not so. Mom started laying into him because now all we had for supper were hot dogs.

Dad angrily grabbed his car keys off the kitchen table, muttered, "Two and six is shit," and headed out the door. Mom, Jackie, and I assumed he was just going to get another can of beans or some cigarettes at the corner store. When dad didn't show until three hours later, all bets were off. Mom wound up giving us hot dogs on white bread, with white bread and butter on the side, yellow Jell-O for dessert. Pissa!

After taking baths, we settled in to watch *The Jackie Gleason Show*. We heard dad's Nash beach wagon pull up. By now, dad's whole demeanor had changed. He breezed into the house singing that Gene McDaniel's song, '*A Hundred Pounds of Clay*,' and headed straight to the kitchen.

I could tell mom was steamed because even though she was looking at the tv, she wasn't laughing at all the appropriate times when Gleason was killing it. After several minutes of doing her best to keep her composure, mom went into the kitchen. Dad was putting the final strips of a one-pound package of bacon on a lit frying pan.

"What are you doing?" mom shrieked, "I defrosted that for Sunday's breakfast!"

Dad said something to the effect that "a man's gotta eat when a man's gotta eat."

Mom wasn't buying dad's ironclad logic and started lighting him up like a Chinese lantern. He headed upstairs towards his bedroom in retreat, only now he was singing that country song, '*Stand by Your Man*.'

The next morning, I was getting ready for nine o'clock Mass and noticed that dad had slept in the same clothes he had on the day before. He seemed real quiet compared to the previous night.

At the Children's Mass, Monsignor Phelan was celebrating, which meant no one would be nodding off during service. Monsignor Phelan was a short, chubby priest who had a booming baritone that sounded like it was shot out of a cannon. His voice pretty much rendered the PA system useless. He would only use it if he had laryngitis or a similar ailment. His sermons almost always centered on siblings "little Johnny and Mary." and his themes varied even less. Johnny would tempt Mary to sin with him and Mary would demure and point Johnny to the light of the Lord. Johnny would see the error of his ways and repent his transgressions to God Almighty.

As predictable as these sermons were, the Monsignor told them with such a dramatic, theatrical flair that it compelled everyone present to hang on his every word, especially the Sisters of St Joseph, God bless them. Why, if you'd listen to the nuns tell it, the Monsignor even gave Cardinal Cushing himself, a run for his money in the charm department. Be that as it may, there was something to be said of the Catholic liturgy. Said mostly in the ancient Latin rite of the Tridentine Mass, English was only uttered during gospel readings, the homily, or when the Monsignor had to correct us for sitting, standing, or kneeling at the wrong times.

Even though I didn't understand the Roman Latin from Pig Latin, there was an undeniable feel and beauty for the cadence of a Mass celebrated in Latin. The language had a rhythm and a reverence that English couldn't duplicate. After the Second Vatican Council a few years later, all this became moot anyways. It was as if the world's Cardinals got together, took all the Masses' most beautiful rites and traditions, and threw them into the air, like they were playing 52 Pickup.

That aside, with about ten minutes left in the Mass, I started to get antsy. I slowly started to rotate my head in complete 360-degree circles. I was obviously distracting the rest of my classmates, because less than five minutes later, Sister Leo the XIII pulled me out of the pew and made me sit with her. Initially embarrassed, that feeling passed about a minute later when I heard the Monsignor give us his blessing and say, "Go in peace, to praise and serve the Lord."

When I got home, mom and dad seemed to have buried the hatchet from the previous night. Dad told mom that he got a great last-minute rental deal on a cottage in Rumney, New Hampshire. This would be the first time we would go away for a week during summer vacation. During the summer we usually went on day trips to some crummy pond on the South Shore. Seemed dad had scored the place from Ritchie Kerrigan, one of his buddies from work, for only sixty bucks for the whole week.

Cripes, that was like ten bucks a night! Back then, sixty bucks and a couple of pounds of bologna went a long way for a family of eight. One of Ritchie's kids had chicken pox and it was starting to spread to all his other kids like wildfire. At first, mom felt a little funny about it, until dad reminded her that, "One man's trash is another man's treasure."

'Nuff said. Now mom was all-in.

We were leaving the following Saturday. All week the house was a whirlwind of preparation and excitement. Before leaving, dad loaded all five of us boys into the wagon for our annual whiffle haircuts at the Barber School in Boston's South End. This was a working barbershop that doubled as a training ground for men who wanted to get certified as barbers. This had to be the largest barbershop in the world because the building sported over sixty chairs spread out over three large connecting rooms.

The best part was that since these students were in training, haircuts only cost fifty cents apiece. Plus, you never had to wait. Even dad got the buzz cut. You do the math. Six haircuts for three bucks and a dollar tip. Mucho score-o!

With his thinning grey hair, dad's new cut made him look more like a psychotic escapee from the Mattapan nuthouse than a former W.W. II jarhead. On occasion, the students would butcher the job, but the saving grace was that you had all summer for it to grow back in.

When Saturday morning arrived, we helped dad overpack the beach wagon and the roof rack with all our clothes and gear. Thank God for dad's side mirrors, because the rearview mirror was rendered useless from all the stuff crammed into the car. Jackie and I called dibs on the third-row seats, which faced the cars behind us.

Barry, Bobby and Mikey sat in the middle with Duchess while mom rode shotgun, holding Patty. Once we got on I-95 it was pretty much clear sailing. We had all the windows open so that Duchess wouldn't get carsick. Dad chain-smoked his Winstons and held steady at seventy m.p.h.

On the way up, Jackie and I were waving to the drivers behind us. They would initially wave back to us, unless we did it to the same driver for too long. Then they would make believe that they didn't see us anymore.

Mom did her best to keep the younger ones engaged by playing "I Spy" and "Billy Button, Who's got the Button?" All in all, the little ones did do a good job of keeping their yelling and fighting to acceptable levels.

Ten miles over the state border, Jackie and I saw the twins sleeping bags blow off the roof rack. Jackie yelled out to tell dad, who just as quickly cut three lanes over to get in the breakdown lane. Once in the breakdown, he gunned it in reverse for nearly a mile till we reached the bags by the side of the road. Surprisingly, they were still in usable condition. We re-secured the sleeping bags to the roof, and arrived at our destination—three hours after leaving the house.

The cottage was more like a hunting cabin than anything else. We had running water, but only cold. The place also had a funky, musty smell that reminded me of grandma's pajamas. The bathroom door had a sign with a poem on it that read: "If it's yellow, let it mellow, if it's brown, flush it down." The younger kids were all running around ape-shit, claiming which bedrooms were theirs. Jackie and I helped dad unload the wagon as mom settled the kids down as best she could.

The cabin also had a cool fireplace with a stack of wood beside it. This being July, I figured we might only need it to roast marshmallows, not realizing that temps could drop forty degrees during the night in the White Mountains. Every cot included a nice army blanket on it.

Aside from the funky smell and wooden furniture everywhere, it was a great place. About the only thing that wasn't made out of wood were the ratty, drab drapes, which served as doors between the rooms. I guess the lack of privacy trade-off was that in the middle of the night Duchess could visit whomever she wanted.

There was a screened-in porch and a big yard with a charcoal grill. Our first night there, dad emptied a can of lighter fluid onto the charcoal and grilled up cheeseburgers and hot dogs. Us kids had the dogs. Dad claimed there was nothing better in the world than a hot dog grilled in the White Mountains, but I didn't think they tasted any different.

After supper, the grease flames died down enough so that now a bright orange glow peeked between the black coals, perfect for roasting marshmallows. All the kids jockeyed for position, trying to get their marshmallow sticks as close to the orange embers as possible. Mom was holding Patty, trying to keep the peace around the grill, while dad hung back chain-smoking and pounding his Colt 45s. Duchess was scrounging the ground under the picnic table where we had just eaten.

When she saw everyone had stopped eating the marshmallows and were just trying to set them on fire, mom broke up the party.

Dad crushed another beer can in his hand and asked us if we wanted to hear a ghost story. Everyone started to squeal in delight when he began his tale. About two minutes in, no one could follow the storyline because he started to lose his train of thought—and his audience.

Mom declared it was time for bed and started to get the younger ones settled in. Jackie and I got into our cots, but dad had one more prank up his sleeve. He stood at our drapes, silently staring at us with a grin like a pie-eyed baboon, and vigorously shook a can of 'Old Foamy' shaving cream. Seconds later, dad lathered Jackie and me up with the same gusto he usually reserved for us while giving us the belt for misbehaving.

Once more mom had to intervene to restore the peace. Ten minutes later, Jackie and I were sound asleep, smelling like a pair of lime rickeys.

Mom and dad had planned a pretty tight itinerary which included three beach days and two side trips. The beach was a nearby lake only a ten-minute drive away. Our first day trip was to a park called *'The Lost Mineshaft.'*

We found out about this place after dad grabbed sightseeing brochures at a gas station where we had stopped to ask directions. The Lost Mineshaft was an attraction set in an old western ghost town where you could mine for gold at Sutter's Mill Creek, ride on a real stagecoach, or even watch a blacksmith shoe a horse. The town's sheriff warned us if we took the stage to be on the lookout for bushwhackers and claim jumpers, who might want to tangle with us. The main attraction was riding in the railroad cart through the Lost Mineshaft itself. It was sort of like riding a slow, herky-jerky roller coaster in a dark building. The track was laid out so that when the ride was over, it dropped you off at the gift shop before you exited the park. Other than inflicting some minor neck pain, it was the park's best ride.

The day nearly went off without a hitch. Mom packed a picnic lunch of chicken loaf and cheese sandwiches with potato salad and cookies for dessert.

"Eat up, all you hungry cowpokes, we've got plenty of sandwiches," she said.

"We'll be eating chicken loaf sandwiches till they're coming out our ass," I absentmindedly blurted. I didn't realize what I said until dad shot me his *you-son-of-a-bitch* look. He would have backhanded me right there if there hadn't been so many witnesses in the picnic area. At four-thirty, dad navigated the Nash out of the parking lot and back down I-95, with a car full of happy, sunburnt prospectors.

We spent the next two days at the lake. It was pretty uneventful, except for the first day when I nearly drowned. It was my entire fault. When we got there I had rushed ahead of the others to be the first in the water. I stepped into a drop and started thrashing around until a fifteen-year-old fat girl pulled me out. This got me a double timeout from mom. One for disobeying her by running ahead, and another for not giving the chicken loaf and cheese sandwich an hour to digest before going into the water.

The next day, we were back on I-95 heading to *'Marty's Trading Post.'* Its main attraction was trained bears. The drive to get there took us an hour and a half because dad overshot the exit and had to turn around. It was also 90 degrees out.

The situation worsened when, just as we were pulling into Marty's parking lot, dad realized he had left his wallet back at the cabin. Well, mom just about blew a gasket and wanted to turn around right then and there. Dad mustered all his charm and on-the-spot-bullshit he could think of so we could at least view the bears from behind a chain-link fence in the parking lot.

The bears were situated on small, wooden platforms that had been built on to trees that didn't have any bark or branches on them. Sort of like a totem pole without the cool Indian artwork. There were five or six bears on three poles. Problem was, none of the bears were hardly moving. Most of them were sleeping. I thought it was because of the heat. Dad scoffed at that notion and said they were trained professionals, just resting up between performances.

After fifteen minutes of viewing the bears, we grabbed about a hundred brochures to attractions that we would never visit and headed back to the cabin. Dad did have another surprise up his sleeve and told us we were going to pass the famed *'Old Man on The Mountain'* on the way back.

A hundred yards of the viewing range, dad announced that we were approaching the sight.

We cried out, "Where?"

"THERE, ON THE RIGHT!" dad shouted.

Dad's right was Jackie's and my left, and the younger ones didn't know left or right from center, so they were looking everywhere except up. It didn't clarify matters either when dad said it was a ten-thousand-year-old natural wonder. Mom marveled at how beautiful The Old Man appeared.

"What? A ten-thousand-year-old, beautiful guy? Where?"

At sixty m.p.h. our window to see this eighth wonder of the world soon closed.

We spent the rest of the vacation cooking out and spending time at the lake. It seemed to me that mom and dad enjoyed relaxing at the lake the most. Mom would wade in the water to supervise and play with us kids. Dad would perch himself in a beach chair under a pine tree, while swigging his Colt 45s and using the beach as an ashtray.

When the spirit did move him, he would grab the giant inner tube and paddle out to the raft. Once there, he would loop a clothesline tied to the raft to his big toe and read the *Daily Racing Form* while bobbing in the water. Dad did cut somewhat of a dandy figure when he was on the beach. He'd wear his knee length, terrycloth Chinese kimono, covered with small images of pagodas and Chinese junks on it, looking like some ancient Oriental warlord.

He had told me he acquired the robe as a war souvenir while fighting in the South Pacific. Mom told me later that she had ordered it through the Sears and Roebuck catalogue as a birthday present for him.

This was the best family vacation we had before we headed home on Saturday. We were really no different from any other family in our neighborhood. No one had any money. We were poor and like the rest of our neighbors, we didn't know it, either…maybe we were naïve, too.

Shortly after arriving home, the Cosgrove twins told us our local golf course was giving caddie lessons on the following Saturday. They said the club was recruiting new caddies and that their dad was making them go sign up. Jackie and I didn't have to twist dad's arm to sell him on the idea. He told us back in his day, his folks sent him away to caddie camp every year in Maine for the whole summer.

Come Saturday, dad dropped us off at the street entrance to the course, not realizing it was another half a mile walk to the clubhouse. When we got to the pro shop, we milled around with another dozen kids, including Vito, who were also there for the lessons. An hour later, a kid around sixteen came out of the pro shop and told us he was Roger Wright, the caddie master, and told us to follow him.

You would have thought Roger had been munching on shit all morning, judging from his attitude. He seemed put off by the fact that teaching some snot-faced kids how to caddie was even in his job description.

Even after he got to know us, Roger was in the habit of always calling everyone by their last name, like you were in the army or something. He took us to the third hole, which he said was an easy par three. He had a wedge with him and started taking a half dozen tee shots to the green. He landed four shots on the green, one over and one into a sand trap off to the left. It seemed more like a golf lesson than a caddie lesson for all the showing off he was doing. We followed him down to the green as he told us about raking out sand traps, divot replacement, fore caddying for ball spotting, and a bunch of other rules governing golf etiquette. Roger did reproach a few of the kids when they started farting around giving each other noogies and Indian arm burns.

Roger ended the lesson after an hour to pass out crappy, mesh baseball caps and baby blue t-shirts to those of us who were still there. He told us to come back at eight o'clock the next day if we were serious about making some scratch.

As Jackie, Vito and I walked home, it dawned on us that the Cosgrove twins had never even showed up.

It only took a few weeks for Jackie and me to pick up the basics of caddying and golf in general. There was a pecking order in caddying that was designated by the letters A, B, and C. A's were rated the highest and C's the lowest. This also determined the pay scale; A caddies got $ 3.50 per bag, B's paid $3.25, and C's paid an even $3.00. This may not sound like much, but if you were an A caddie, and carried two bags per loop, you would usually make $9.00 a round, $7.00 scale and another $2.00 in tips. In today's dollars, that equates to around $400. bucks a day after you adjust for inflation.

You moved up or down the pay steps depending on getting either good or bad reviews from the golfers you looped for. Being in Roger's good graces also could move you up the caddie ladder quicker. Both Jackie and I were A caddies in no time.

However, my top status as an A caddie was short-lived.

One day, Roger sent me out to loop for Nerves Norton and Packie Downes, and it didn't go well. Although Packie could hold his own in match play, Nerves was another story completely. The kids called him, *'Nerves'* due to his uncontrollable arm-shaking during his backswing. Not a good thing when you're playing five bucks Nassau against a couple of scratch golfers.

Anyways, we got to the twelfth, where a notorious marsh encroaches the hole. Sure enough, Nerves goes into his shaking backswing and lets one rip— right into the five-foot-high reeds. That one was gone and Nerves blamed me for losing it. He got so upset he splintered his driver right there on the tee markers.

Nerves and Packie lost a bundle against their opponents that day. Aside from having to use a three-wood off the tees the rest of the way, he didn't speak to me the rest of the round. He did however give Roger an earful about me when we were finished. Nerves even ratted me out for smoking at one of the forecaddie holes, although it was the other caddie in the loop.

Roger, in turn, let me have it in the back of the pro shop where the caddies collected their pay. He read me the riot act and gave me a two-week suspension to boot. Dad was understandably furious when I broke the news to him back home. "Get in the car, NOW," dad commanded.

On the drive back to the course, I asked, "What should I say to Roger?" "You tell that little piss-pot that you can't afford a two-week suspension, Period!" Dad snorted.

Dad made it to the rear of the pro shop parking lot in record time. He waited for me as I went over to the Dutch door and rang the bell. Roger came to the door and asked me what I wanted.

"My father told me to tell you, that I can't afford a two-week suspension, Period." I answered.

Roger looked up and saw my dad seething in the hot car, glaring at him. He looked back at me and said, "Okay, McCauley, suspension rescinded. You can come back tomorrow, but I'm busting you to a C."

I was back in, but being a C caddie was the equivalent of caddie purgatory. In addition to assigning me just one bag per loop instead of doubles, Roger also had the option of pairing me with some of the cheapest pikers with the heaviest bags in the club. If he really had a hair across his ass, he might even loop me with some of the lousiest women hackers on the course.

About a week after I was busted, Roger looped me with Mucka McGrew. Besides the illegal number of clubs in his bag and his thirty-five handicap, Mucka always wore the same smelly, black golf shirt with the little green alligator on it. They called him "Mucka" for the giant gobs of tobacco chew he'd stick in his mouth and spit out. When he did hit a good shot, which wasn't often, he'd get excited and the spittle would dribble down his chin. You'd have thought you were watching Rod Carew taking batting practice the way his cheek ballooned out. It also wasn't advisable to be caught downwind of Mucka when it was time to let some of that nasty stuff fly.

On this particular day, it must have been a hundred and ten by the time we got to the tenth tee, where there was a canteen truck. It was customary for the golfers to take a ten-minute break at this midpoint and to spring for hot dogs and cold sodas for themselves and their caddies.

Mind you, I didn't want to blame it on heat exhaustion, but I made the mistake of sitting beside Mucka on the bench and, after he wolfed his dog down, he asked for a bite of mine. I hesitantly passed him my dog and damn, if he didn't inhale half that wiener in one bite, and left what was left of it dripping in tobacco juice. I got up and discreetly tossed the rest of the dog away, under the pretense of fiddling with Mucka's clubs in his bag.

It wasn't all doom and gloom at the course, however. We got through it, as we always did. The membership valued their caddies enough so that they allowed us to golf for free every Monday afternoon. They also organized a caddie day outing for us to an amusement park in New Hampshire, all expenses paid. They even got us a Greyhound bus for the round trip.

This being my first time travelling first class and all, I continually played with the recline button on my armrest, so that my seat kept going up and down. Unbeknownst to me, I was whacking my old neighborhood nemesis, Kevin Cullen, on his knees with every downward motion. After crashing his kneecaps once too often, Kevin stuck his face over my headrest and said, "Do that once more, McCauley, and I'm gonna play '*Wipe Out*' on your head." Message received. As it was, I think Kevin would have smacked me right then if a couple of chaperones hadn't been sitting directly behind him.

That day we had a blast. I must have ridden the Yankee Cannonball roller coaster thirteen times. To top it off, no one was mistakenly left at the park or puked on the bus on the way home. As far as my caddying skills went, I wasn't the best and I wasn't the worst, although I never was able to adequately explain to dad how I once caddied for a one-armed golfer and didn't pick up on it until the tenth hole. I must have been thinking of starting high school the following week or something.

After eight years of Catholic instruction in parochial school I would be transitioning to four years of Catholic instruction at Don Bosco High School. The only difference being this was an all-boys private school, run by the Salesians of Don Bosco (S.D.B.). The school's joke was that S.D.B. really stood for, "send dollar bills." They had a curriculum that was half vocational and half college courses.

On the vocational side, I was enrolled in the Building Technologies Program, otherwise known as Woodworking 101. Not knowing the difference between a rip saw and a bag of hammers, I figured my shop instructor had his work cut out for him with me. The man charged with honing our wood-challenged skills was Brother Julius, a sixty-year-old Italian master carpenter.

Brother Julius had fingers the width of your big toes and hands as coarse as number-three sandpaper. Small in stature, but a giant in his field, even the shortest kid in shop stood nearly a head over him. His beige lab coat carried to his knees with pockets so wide and deep, they looked like a toolbox could get lost in them.

With his heavy Italian accent and thick, black frame glasses, he could have passed for a mad scientist gone AWOL from a sci-fi movie. He wore his shock of silver hair slicked back in a tapered, steel mane. His look was topped off with a left eye made of glass— not unlike a doll's eye— unblinking, forever fixed. How and when he acquired it, no one knew, which only fired our unbridled imaginations even more. Shop accident? Birth defect? Knife fight? No one ever had the nerve to ask.

Despite any physical limitations we may have seen in our mentor, Brother Julius displayed not an ounce of self-pity for his condition, and even less interest in what we thought. His passion and dedication for teaching us the craft was beyond reproach. As skilled as he was with either hand or power tool, he wasn't averse to using discipline if you fell behind your classmates, or were guilty of some other shop infraction. He would employ the blunt end of a hand tool to your midsection just as easily as using his fist like a mallet to your chin, Moe Howard style. It was the type of relationship we had with most of the teachers, based on respect and a healthy dose of fear.

Our first shop exercise was making a mortise and tenon. These were two small pieces of wood that—after being properly measured and chiseled—would fit snugly into one another when coupled together. After two weeks of ignoring the carpenter's credo to "measure twice and cut once," I finally had a mortise and tenon that didn't overlap and held firmly at any angle. It wasn't until I completed the project that I noticed one piece of pinewood was about a half a foot longer than the other. This gave the mortise and tenon the appearance of the cross. Perhaps the project was designed also to have a subliminal religious lesson.

Shortly after passing them in to be graded, Brother Julius passed them all back to us. We were scratching our heads after seeing there were no physical grade markings on them. Brother then picked up my mortise as he walked by my workbench and held it up high for all to see.

"Dis 'ere right 'ere, is a piece of junk," he declared in his best broken- English to my fellow wood heads. "You may think it's a piece of art… but it's junk," he stated again, this time more gratuitously. He walked over to the trash barrel that we used for our woodworking mistakes, and casually tossed it in. Whether he was singling out my mortise for its lack of craftsmanship, or just choosing anyone's piece indiscriminately, I never knew. Maybe I was afraid to know.

It was either through the power of osmosis or the threat of being on the business end of a hand tool that by senior year our carpentry skills came into sharp focus. Our year-end project would be building office desks.

Brother unlocked the supply room where he stored his choicest maple and oak stock, along with some of the finest Formica money could buy. We proceeded to chisel, rout, and band saw our way into creating twenty of the sharpest-looking desk sets we could fashion. We drenched our creations in polyurethane, formicaed our desktops in pale green and accented the drawers with wrought iron hardware. These desks were tricked out with seven drawers, three over three on each side, with a wide and narrow middle drawer that could store a boatload of stationary sundries.

Just as we were finishing up our projects, Brother Julius informed us that we would not be allowed to purchase these desks for ourselves. Although it had always been a past practice to do so for the price of the stock, this year our school had committed to donating them to a new wing of the Deer Island Reform School, outside of Boston. Pissa!

For all his peculiarities, Brother Julius taught us well and did instill in us a sense of pride and confidence as potential millwrights.

Woodworking was a welcome afternoon diversion after a morning of all the college courses, including Father Angelo's trigonometry class. Father Angelo did triple duty as the school's math and gym teacher, plus cheerleading coach. He tended to use his physical prowess in the gym as an analogy to the mental sharpness required for solving mathematical equations—the difficulty of the problem notwithstanding. Since I excelled at dodgeball more than the applied principles of mathematical logic, it wasn't a surprise that I preferred the former to the latter. That being said, I could feel myself starting to panic when I heard Father Angelo utter those four cringeworthy words, "McCauley... to the board!"

There but for the grace of God, I imagined my trig-challenged classmates thinking. I rose slowly from my seat and proceeded to the blackboard as if I was on a one-man, Bataan Death March.

"Master McCauley," he began, "prove to your fellow mathematical misfits how those triangles are congruent."

After feigning some unintelligible mutterings about ninety-degree angles and the requisite amount of head scratching, Father Angelo saw through my ruse and said resignedly, "Sit down, you intellectual infant, and let another one of your classmates step up and shine like Pythagoras himself."

Ruefully, the same sorry scenario played out with a few more of my classmates before the bell mercifully rang, signaling a classroom change.

These class changes were remarkably efficient in relation to the number of students all scurrying around at the same time. They owed their sense of orderliness and propriety to one figure: Father Dmitri Stanislaus, or "The Slaw," as the plebs called him. Fifty percent Russian, fifty percent Polish, and a hundred percent badass. How this guy ever got out of the seminary was anyone's guess. He was the school's Dean of Discipline, who brokered respect from everyone, and bullshit from no one.

He stood in the hallway like a silent sentry, a human cornerstone thrust between two of the school's busiest intersections. His mere presence was enough to ensure a seamless transition between one classroom to the next. God help the pupil who reckless or stupid enough to take the Slaw's baleful glare and return it back to him, let alone cause a hall disturbance.

This day, a few sophomores made the mistake of engaging in loud behavior that the Slaw wouldn't let pass. It wasn't half a minute after the horseshit started, that it was over. The Slaw brought it to a fleeting conclusion by slamming both kids into the lockers. In addition to them falling ass over teakettle, he also slapped them with a Saturday detention.

Saturday jug wasn't falling asleep in some unattended classroom either. Having committed a minor indiscretion myself as a freshman, I was privy to how Saturday detentions worked. On First Fridays of every month, the student body would march the short distance from our school to the Cathedral of the Holy Cross to celebrate Mass. Being uninitiated to the protocols early in the school year, I ill-advisedly skipped out of church with the seniors at the conclusion of the service, as they were being dismissed first. In hindsight, I don't think I had finished enjoying my third cigarette on the bus ride home before I was busted. I found out the following Monday morning in the principal's office that the Slaw had taken attendance right after he dismissed the seniors, giving me plenty of rope with which to hang myself.

When I reported to Saturday jug, one of the brothers armed me with a butter knife, took me to the student chapel and had me scrape the wax remnants out of all the glass candleholders on the altar. I also was tasked with scraping all the glasses that were in the Devotional Candle Stand, and those must have numbered in the thousands. It could have been worse. They could have had me mopping floors and washing chalk-caked blackboards. At lunchtime, they brought me with them to dine in their private residences. I can attest to the fact that those guys ate pretty well, too. This detention did provide me at least one unintended benefit. It allowed me to get to know many of the brothers and priests on a more personal level. Many of these men were the upperclassmen teachers, and now they knew me by my first name.

Aside from restoring order to these corridors of serenity, the Slaw's over-the-top reaction also served as a warning to any would-be troublemakers who were going to be walking those halls for the next few years.

If that wasn't warning enough, you always could take a cue from the seniors whenever they sang, "I Fought the Slaw and the Slaw Won." Although the discipline could be viewed as somewhat archaic in terms of the living room psychology employed in classrooms today, nothing could be further from the truth. The uniformity and regimentation of the day provided us with an *esprit de corps* and a sense of discipline that would serve us well in our future endeavors.

Besides, it wasn't as if they left any marks on us, at least not physically. As we were told by one of the prefects during freshman orientation, our high school years would be the fastest in our lives. Despite Father Angelo's math classes, they were. Graduation day came and the ceremony would be held in St. James Church. It wasn't known until sometime later that one of the seniors who had been expelled the previous January for shoplifting, attempted to exact his revenge by setting the church on fire. His M.O. was to empty a can of lighter fluid on the heavy, maroon drapes on the confessional box, and then torching them. He would have been spotted sooner, but he had snuck inside the church before the graduates had gathered in the vestibule. His ploy was partly foiled by a church usher who quickly doused the blaze with a fire extinguisher, but not before the drapes were toast.

The culprit had only suffered superficial, first-degree burns to his hands and neck. After the arsonist was bandaged and cuffed by police, he was taken away and the ceremony resumed without further incident. Thankfully, the fire was extinguished in time for the graduation to go on as scheduled. Twenty minutes later, nearly everyone had forgotten about the smell that permeated the sanctuary from the smoldering drapes.

Part 2

It wasn't long after graduation that many of the guys from the old neighborhood joined a local social club called The Boot. It had served the community as a small diner for several years before going out of business. Prior to that, it had been known as The Boot and Shoe, a cobbler shop run by the same Italian family for about three generations. Its identity was so ingrained in the neighborhood that it retained its name no matter what business was there.

After the restaurant went out of business, the city took possession when it didn't sell and its previous owner stopped paying its taxes. Several pillars of the community got together and were able to purchase it for short money as a place to socialize and to ostensibly perform charitable works in the neighborhood.

Initially, the members would hold semi-annual paper drives, ring bells at Christmas for the Salvation Army, or help out with the fireworks for the Fourth.

By the time my crew was coming in, the club was volunteering less and socializing more. Membership to the club was cheap, too. Twenty bucks a year got you a pool table, a large color tv, and a few red leather couches. The *pièce de résistance* was a bar that featured fifty-cent drafties and a buck for a bottle of beer. Nice.

The Boot wasn't without its share of shenanigans and misadventures over the years either. There was the night Wacko Halloran snuck up behind a drunken Leo Rohner, playing in an all-night card game, and feigned giving him a golden shower.

To this day his motive is unknown, but as I recall, Wacko was working a pretty good buzz that night himself. Wacko snuck up behind Leo, stood up on a folding chair, dropped his jeans and held an open bottle of cream soda in front of his crouch, unleashing a steady stream of the liquid gold onto Leo.

By the time Leo stood and staggered around to face Wacko, the soda bottle had been tossed in a corner—leaving Leo staring at

Wacko's underpants. The ruse was aided by the other card players who started overreacting as to how grossed out they all were.

Naturally, Leo jumped to the only conclusion he could, albeit a drunken one. Wacko bolted lickety-split. Leo tried to pivot out of his chair to give chase and tripped over the chair's leg, knocking himself out cold on the floor.

A few players joked about reviving Leo by pouring more cream soda over his face. Instead, after someone played *'Mack the Knife'* on the jukebox, we noticed that Leo's right foot started to move, and then tapped to the beat of the song. Seconds later, he was sitting up on the floor asking, "What happened?" When Leo became coherent enough, someone asked him what he had been mixing his vodka with. No one was really surprised when the answer came back, "Saliva!"

The Boot did pride itself on some of the innovative ploys it came up with over the years to help sustain it. One year the club held a raffle called the *'Bug of Booze.'* The grand prize was a new Volkswagen Bug filled with cases of beer and liquor. Initially, we wanted a Volkswagen bus, but after doing the math, the price of the booze alone would have been prohibitive.

Still, after purchasing the Bug and the booze, we figured we'd still profit over two grand if early tickets sales were any indication. The only issue was, two days prior to the drawing date, we entrusted Wacko to pick up the vehicle at the VW dealership. Big mistake. After Wacko left the car lot, he stopped at a 7-11 to buy a pack of butts. He left the keys in the car and when he came back out, the keys were gone … along with the spanking new VW Bug.

Three days later, when the police found the car across town in a chop shop, the only part not stripped down or fenced was the cigarette lighter. Back at the Boot, we gathered up the raffle stubs, contacted all the contestants to reimburse them, and drank away the other half of the prize to console ourselves.

The following summer, the members planned a deep sea fishing trip in the seaport town of Plymouth, fifty miles away. We made arrangements to charter out the *Capt'n Billy*, a forty-footer with twin diesels. The boat provided all the fishing gear and bait we would need.

When the day arrived, we loaded our cars with several cases of beer and cold-cut subs and headed south. We arrived on the docks by 7:00 a.m. and a half hour later were heading towards Minot Light, drinks in hand. We initiated betting pools for the smallest, largest, and first fish caught. Unfortunately, it wasn't long before alcohol combined with the ocean's motion had several of us heading for the john in the galley down below.

Aside from the few cases of seasickness, everything was going great until around one o'clock. It was just after everyone had eaten lunch and the *Capt'n Billy* had dropped anchor where radar had picked up a large school of fish.

One of the guys had brought aboard a gallon of Seagram's Seven Crown, and started to pass it around in little white cups. I don't think that jug was more than half gone when the trip started going south. A half dozen of the more drunken buffoons started to peel off their clothes and jump overboard—ripped and stripped. This brought jeers and catcalls from the rest of those onboard. A few more guys started to toss their fishing gear into the deep. Minutes later, they were throwing whatever wasn't tied down overboard. It was a mutiny without a cause. The Captain shot out of his wheelhouse, grabbed his mate and started to throw life jackets to the guys, some of whom were now struggling to stay afloat.

After the Captain and his mate had successfully fished all the drunks out of the drink, he pulled anchor, fired up his twins, and headed back to shore. Party over!

From the stern, I looked back and saw a debris field of floating fishing gear: poles, tackle boxes, life jackets, chum buckets, and Styrofoam beer coolers. Everything was bobbing in a jagged line of flotsam and jetsam. About a mile from shore, we could see the flashing blue lights of half a dozen Plymouth police cars, waiting for us on the dock.

Incredibly, after docking, the Captain tallied up a bill for his lost or damaged equipment, talked it over with the harbormaster and police chief, and gave us the option between jail time or settling up. We paid the damages and were told never to return to Plymouth again, essentially earning a lifetime ban for thirty jackasses. A hard lesson learned when you mix Seagram's Seven with the seven seas.

Despite all-night card games, well-intentioned raffles, and bad fishing trips, the Boot was a wonderful place to socialize and make long-lasting friendships. After a few years, I think some of us were tiring of the nightly routine. Like the rest of my friends, I was investing my finances in gambling and my health in alcohol. Jackie was getting bored too, but for a different reason. Aside from the tedium, Jackie was also getting burnt out from working as a middle school substitute teacher.

Who could blame him? Three years in as a sub with no foreseeable prospect of securing tenure? Plus, subbing was just a stopgap to hold the fort until the regular teacher got back from sick leave. And most of the teachers were getting sick from teaching. Sadly, subbing was always more about babysitting than actual teaching. Near the end of his third year, Jackie's principal called him in for his annual review.

Sensing a marked difference in his attitude and his overall disinterest with substituting in general, he asked Jackie why he had ever started teaching in the first place.

"Two reasons: July and August," Jackie cracked. To no one's surprise, Jackie wasn't called back for a fourth year.

By the same token, I wasn't making a lot of progress career wise as an order picker for Sears and Roebuck. It started out as a part-time Christmas gig, but they must have seen something in me they liked because they kept me on as a full-timer after the holiday season ended. Basically, I was working off a conveyor belt, placing Sears products into alphabetically labeled bins, determined by a customer's last name. A sweeper on the opposite side of the bin would box the product for shipping and then slide the product to a cashier who would apply the invoice and address to the box. Dad used to tease me that it was no different than separating jellybeans at Woolworths, but I never saw the correlation. Of course, dad would have ragged me if I had been making a million bucks a year.

Still, after a few years I was starting to tire of the job. Even the Grog was getting a bit old. The Grog was a local Irish bar that served up weekend doses of good Irish/Country music with bad barroom food to a mostly Gaelic clientele. The house band was Little Dan Teehan and his Irish Showband. Why, Dan would have you nearly crying in your fish and chips after singing his signature song, '*Noreen Bawn.*' The band almost always closed with this song. Dan's soaring rendition of this melancholy ballad would turn the rowdiest of the Gaelic lads into teary-eyed Sons of the Old Brigade, arm in arm, comrades all. At its conclusion, they would be just as content to revert back to form and beat the piss out of you once outside.

They weren't the only ones, either. Praise be to the saints if you were tempted to start any monkey business with other patrons or the bartenders themselves. They could hurdle that bar in their black ties and dress whites and pound your ass before the foam had time to settle on your pint. According to some of the bartenders, pummeling their patrons with impunity was one of the jobs best bennies.

Despite all this, the Grog was still the place to be, come weekend nights. It was crowded, loud, and fun. Where else could you rub elbows with a middleweight boxer or a parched big city mayor coming in for a cold one after last call? Where else could you meet Irish colleens as pretty and pure as morning dew or who could turn the king's language saltier than the Grog's stale pretzels? They could be sweet as pie or as shrill as a shrew, especially if they felt you were "dragging you boots" when it came time to order them up another Vodka Collins. In short, these daughters of Erin were wonderful.

On one such night, Jackie and I struck up a conversation with two pretty lasses who asked us to join them in their booth. They told us they came from County Clare. Jackie countered by declaring, "Aye good ladies, we hail from County Cork, as we are both a couple of cork suckers." Despite Jackie's bad brogue and even worse play on words, the girls laughed hard and took no offense. Actually, one of the girls countered with her own brand of raunchy humor. "What's grosser than grease on Olivia Newton John?" she queried.

"I don't know. What?" I asked.

'*Come on Eileen*,' she laughed out loud.

We continued in this manner drinking, laughing, and telling lies, little and large. If we were reluctant to join them in a lively two-step jive, they would dance with each other. It was just another loud, lively night at the Grog. Little did we suspect that Jackie would one day marry one of these girls and I would date the other one off and on over the next few years.

Jackie's future bride's name was Nora Gallagher, a green-carder who had a body as stout and robust as a freshly poured pint of Guinness. With raven-black hair and dancing blue eyes, she told us she had placed third in the last annual *'Rose of Tralee'* beauty pageant.

Mine was Carla Ellison, with hazel eyes and a disposition as sunny and bright as her strawberry-blond hair. She was exuberant, sassy, and just plain fun. She had the unfounded idealism of a hippie and an absence of pretense that would make a hanging judge blush. She found gloom nowhere and optimism everywhere. Her mood ring was perpetually fixed on pink, denoting her ever-present cheery and happy nature. Despite these endearing qualities, I dated other girls over the next few years, but I always came back to Carla.

The only thing that annoyed me about Carla was her general lack of sports knowledge, especially Boston's. She confused baseball's grand slam with a breakfast at Denny's, and in hockey, she called a face off, a "puck off." Forget about the game's greatest names: Williams, Russell, and Orr! I may as well have been talking about some law firm. When it came to her favorite soccer team, the Sligo Rovers Football Club, she could cite you chapter and verse on the team's history, players, records, and all the mundane statistics that accompany it.

Jackie, meanwhile, found career employment with the utilities and started dating Nora on a steady basis. At that stage in my life, I hadn't a clue as to what I wanted. "Young, dumb and full of cum," to quote dad.

Like a rudderless ship absent a sexton, I felt I was afloat in a purposeless ocean, drifting aimlessly in a sea of nothingness.

I started reminiscing about the religious retreats my old high school used to have. Not to suggest that I derived anything remotely profound from these spiritual exercises, but they did usually bring me some measure of inner contentment. If nothing else, the retreats afforded one the opportunity to take a step back, recharge your batteries and refocus on what was really meaningful in your life. Perhaps if I had taken the refocusing part more seriously, I would have had more direction at this stage in my life.

I also recalled Brother Mickey, my high school's track coach giving me "the talk" about vocations in my senior year. This was probably worse than having "the talk" about sex. Initially feeling self-conscious and employing sophomoric one-word answers as my defense, I began to lower my guard the more he talked to me.

"Tommy, have you given any serious consideration about your future after you graduate?" Brother asked.

"Not really," I replied, trying to mask any emotion I might display. "Well," he continued, "I've known you since you were on the freshman squad and I've noticed you have qualifications that would serve you well in any endeavor you may pursue. You possess character, integrity and an even-tempered disposition, all worthy virtues if you ever had an inclination to toil in the service of Our Lord."

"Toil?" I lamely repeated.

"Or minister, if you prefer?" Brother intoned. "Of course, what I'm really inferring is that you prayerfully reflect on leaving your heart open to the voice of Jesus. In other words, don't be afraid to listen to your heart. Do you understand what I'm saying, or do you have any questions?"

"Yes, Brother, I know what you mean, but I did have one question. Do priests really get to take out the parish Cadillac every Wednesday to go golfing?"

"Well Tommy, I think you're confusing priests with doctors who have in fact, designated Wednesdays as their dedicated day to hit the links. As for Cadillacs, I think it's safe to say that most parish vehicles are probably Chevys or Fords and are generally used in the performance of one's priestly duties, golf excursions notwithstanding."

"Thanks Brother, I'll think about it."

Well, a few years later, I was thinking about it. On this night, I was driving Carla from the Grog, and we stopped at the beach before heading home. I don't know if she was in a mood because her beloved Rovers had been eliminated from the league's title match earlier that week, or if it was that time on the calendar for her. Didn't matter. She was lighting me up like a twi-light doubleheader at Fenway.

"What's the matter with you? What's going on? You haven't said anything all night. Are you still seeing other girls?" she demanded.

"Maybe I've got a roving eye and a restless heart," I countered. "Roving hands and a restless dick would be more like it," she retorted. "Now then Carla," I said, "would ye be French-kissing your own mother with that very mouth?" A pause, and before she could slug me the silence was broken by the loud, staccato strains of the Roger Williams version of '*Born Free*' coming over the radio. "Ba, bum… Bum, bum, bum… Ba, ba, bum." I listened to the pounding piano chords pulsating in my ears, along with its hypnotic driving drumbeat. I started miming all the piano parts of the tune on the dashboard, every note timed perfectly. Never before had a song spoken to me with such conviction and purpose. It's soaring melody and lyrics were a triumph of the spirit, uplifting and inspirational, all at once.

Carla thought I was nuts, but I figured I was having the wackiest epiphany since St. Paul was struck down on the road to Damascus. The song was liberating me—from my job, my home, my relationships, from everything. I decided right then and there, I was going to go into the seminary. I actually felt like I was finally '*Born Free*' to praise and serve the Lord. Carla looked at me like I had lost my marbles and seemed more confused than angry about my declaration.

"Are you sure this is what you want to do?" she cried. "You've hardly given it any thought. What about us dating for the past two years? What about your family? Your job? What about me? What about … us?"

The next day at the breakfast table, I excitedly told the family of my decision. They seemed to be all in, expect for dad, who seemed skeptical about the whole idea. Mom, on the other hand was thrilled. Jackie and I made plans to celebrate that night after work at the Grog, even though it was a weeknight. Later that day, I called St. Francis seminary and got a preliminary entrance interview with the director for the very next day. That night at the Grog, with the place half empty, we got our favorite waitress Irene, to serve us. I told Irene of my decision, she congratulated me and started to take our orders. Jackie ordered a pitcher of Guinness.

"I'll have a pitcher, also," I said. "Yeah, but what kind?" Irene inquired. "You know," I stated matter-of-factly.

"I know you'd drink piss out of a sock," Irene deadpanned. "Okay," I said, "gimme a pitcher of lager, any brand."

As Irene went to the bar to fill the orders, Jackie told me that he and Nora had got engaged the night before, but didn't mention it to the family for fear of spoiling my big news. He told me Nora was late—and not with her rent—and they wanted to get married sooner rather than later. He explained they had been talking marriage even before they found out she was pregnant, so this only hastened their decision.

"Well then, now we've got plenty to celebrate," I stated. Irene returned, struggling with our giant pitchers of brew that obscured half her body. The quicker we drained the pitchers, the quicker we lost track of time and the importance of my big interview the following day. When we heard last call, we got up to settle with Irene and said our goodbyes.

When we left the Grog, Jackie and I decided to get some chow at the Hazelwood Diner, an old school, fifties-style hash house right out of a Mickey Spillane novel. Built a generation before, the Hazelwood retained its yesteryear charm with its chrome accents, Formica countertops, and red leather booths.

Proprietor, short order cook, and chief bottle and pot washer, big Jim Bouley was at his station when we arrived, working eight orders at once on his grease-caked grill. These midnight culinary forays to *'The Hazel'* were usually driven by alcohol consumption and the entertainment value of watching a three-hundred-pound guy work his magic on a two-by-four-foot griddle.

Jim Bouley was one of those rare guys who could speed-feed a diner full of tipsy customers and keep a witty conversation going with half the patrons at the same time. He could talk sports, politics, or religion with an equal measure of knowledge and sarcasm. The visit wasn't complete if he hadn't insulted you at least once during your stay. Knowing our orders before we were completely settled in, he had our coffees in front of us before we had our jackets off.

Returning to the grill, he grabbed two sirloin strips out of the small fridge, broke a couple of eggs and had them cooking in ten seconds. Jackie and I sipped our coffees and watched Jim, metal spatula in hand, begin to flip burgers, toast bread, and beat eggs. Our biggest concerns were that Jim's forehead sweat beads didn't accidently garnish our steaks.

Jim was dishing his normal array of sports talk, street gossip, and insults as Jackie and I wolfed down our steak and eggs. Trying to break Jim's momentum and concentration away from the grill, Jackie uncharacteristically ordered a donut. Jim instinctively smelled a rat. Turning away from his grill, he lifted the plastic cover off of the pastry case, grabbed a plain donut, placed it on its side and with a deft wrist flick, rolled it down his soup-stained counter. Like a bartender sliding a mug of beer down a long bar in an old-time western saloon, the donut came to an abrupt stop in front of Jackie before it fell on its side.

"Well played, sir," Jackie conceded.

"Touché, indeed." Jim grinned, and returned to his grill.

After paying our fifteen-dollar tab, we said our "good nights" and drove home. After looking in the fridge for absolutely no other reason than being drunk, I went over to ride the stair lift to my bedroom on the second floor. The stair lift had been installed a month before, when my granddad came to live with us for good. Gramps had gotten a little punch drunk the last few months, and even dad had to admit that he seemed to have lost a few feet off his fastball lately. I figured the only reason I took the lift was because I was too drunk to climb the stairs. Needless to say, dad wasn't thrilled to find me fast asleep, still perched on the lift the next morning at eight o'clock.

He roused me from my stupor and reminded me that my interview was only an hour and a half away. I staggered to the shower, dotted my eyes with Visine, brushed my teeth, got dressed and ate.

I was on the road by nine o'clock flat. The seminary was only five miles from home, but my '73 Plymouth Satellite only had three miles worth of gas in its tank. I was able to pull over to the side of the road just as my car came to a coughing, sputtering halt. I exited the vehicle, feeling like I had blown the interview, when providence intervened.

Directly across the street was a makeshift memorial for some poor soul who had recently been killed while driving his bike on that very spot. In commemoration of his earthly life, his family and friends had gathered flowers, balloons, and stuffed animals and had placed a stark-white, ghost bike in the middle of it all, as its centerpiece. With only fifteen minutes until the interview, I offered up a fast Hail Mary for the dearly departed and "borrowed" the bike for the rest of the trip.

I pulled up to St. Francis with five minutes to spare. The seminary was set on fifty acres of bucolic beauty. The buildings were nestled among hundred-foot ponderosa pines and gentle rolling hills. A slight, middle-aged friar who introduced himself as Brother Leonardo, private secretary to Father Patterson, greeted me at the castle-like structure. He was somewhat of a squirrelly fellow, a no-nonsense sort who seemed to possess about as much charm as the Berlin Wall. He also was burdened with a deformed right leg that must have been a good foot shorter than his left one. His condition had previously necessitated the services of a shoemaker who had cobbled together a special shoe that had a ten-inch heel on it. It was the type of prosthetic contraption that I would have found humorous only a few months earlier.

He took me down a long hall to an office and told me I would be interviewing with the seminary's Prefect and Director of Admissions, Father Francis X. Patterson. After introducing me to Father Patterson, he turned to walk away, dragging his right leg behind him. Father Patterson had been a Franciscan priest for the past twenty-odd years and had been charged with guiding the seminary for the last twelve. He wore hooded brown robes, with a white belt fastened around his waist that looked like a rope. Draped around his neck was a large black crucifix. He had a countenance one would expect of a man of the cloth. His demeanor reflected a man who projected an inner peace, manifested by a life dedicated to the service of Jesus.

He brought me into his office, constructed of dark-paneled walnut and surrounded by the religious artifacts and icons you would expect to find in such an environment. When we were both seated at his desk, he told me a little about himself, seminary life in general, and then asked me the money question, "Why do you want to become a Franciscan priest?"

The question threw me for a moment before I collected my thoughts and replied, "Change, Father. I don't like the changes I've noticed in the church, the country or the world at large. Nothing is the same and it's not as if it's for the better, either. The political upheaval in our country has affected our civility, our culture and has left all our institutions under attack. It's as if everything is upside down and the planet is ready to explode. I don't consider myself superstitious, Father, but it seems like the world's been on this downward spiral ever since the Jets won the Superbowl. I find it confusing and distressing and, as clichéd as it may sound, I would prefer to be a part of the solution rather than be part of the problem."

He seemed to suppress a wry smile before replying, "My son, have you ever heard of the parable of the two boats?"

"No sir," I said. "What's that?"

He leaned forward in his oversized red leather swivel chair, which had a back that stretched a ridiculous five feet over his head, and said, "When I was a teenager, I used to drive my bike past a body of water on my way to my job at a mattress factory every day. There were always two boats anchored near the shoreline. Every day, despite the different weather patterns governing the tides, winds and currents, the positions of the two boats would change, but they wouldn't change. Do you know what I mean?"

"Not really," I confessed. "How can something change, but not change?" I asked.

"Suffice it to say that the more things change, the more they stay the same," he said. "In a similar manner, although there have been several changes in the liturgy since the Second Vatican Council, the core doctrines and dogmas of the church have remained constant for over two thousand years. So, in a sense, it changes, yet it doesn't. Is that any clearer now, my son?"

"Kind of," I hesitantly answered, unconvincingly.

We talked in general terms for ten minutes, and then he told me that the current class of seminarians were completing their formations and were to be ordained in two weeks. He invited me to join them in their final two weeks to get acquainted with "the life" and see if it was compatible to me. He said it would also serve as a probationary period and would allow me some time to prayerfully reflect on the priesthood as a vocation. If all went well, I could formally apply for the upcoming class in the fall.

I didn't find out until later, but after I had left, Father Patterson buzzed his secretary, Brother Leonardo, into his office. He gave him the rundown on me and told him, "Mr. McCauley will be joining the other seminarians for the next two weeks. I want you to keep a very close eye on him."

When I got home, I gave my immediate notice to Sears and tied up some other loose ends, one of which was saying goodbye to Carla. Carla told me she had had a little more time to absorb my decision, and assured me that she loved me too much to try to stand in the way. She reasoned it was a personal decision and mine alone to make. I suppose I was being somewhat selfish, because I did feel a little hurt that she wasn't carrying on by crying or pleading with me to change my mind. In a rare moment of self-reflection, I realized that although I was losing a great girl, I would hopefully be gaining a little humility that was sorely lacking in my wretched being.

After packing a suitcase, I reported at St. Francis the next day at six- thirty in time for daily Mass. I was to be immersed in every facet of the program that the current seminarians were undergoing.

I was given a strict schedule that I was to follow to the letter. Rise and dress at six, Mass at six-thirty, breakfast at seven-thirty, classes eight 'til two-thirty with a half hour for lunch, break between two-thirty and five for homework and downtime, Gregorian chant from five-thirty to six, dinner 'til six-thirty, evening Mass from six-thirty 'til seven-thirty, free time from seven-thirty 'til nine, lights out at nine.

The course load? Theology, Philosophy, Thomasic Theory, Political Science with Major British Writers for dessert. Despite being three years removed from the rigors and discipline of studying in high school, the thought of carrying such a burdensome curriculum was somewhat negated by the fact that it would only be for two weeks. I was ready and rearing.

In addition to all these activities, I was asked to help out with the weekly parish Bingo games. There was also the matter of lending a hand in preparing for a cookout that the school planned for the graduating class and their families two days prior to their Ordination.

I got acclimated to the seminarian's rigid lifestyle fairly quickly due in part to the fullness of the schedule, which in turn made the two weeks fly by. On the day before Ordination, when the seminarians were to take their vows of Holy Orders, I was summoned to Father Patterson's office.

When I entered, Father was standing behind his desk, hands clasped behind his back, staring out his large picture window. While still gazing at the lush rolling hills on the campus, he instructed me to have a seat. I noticed and nodded over to Brother Leonardo, who sat off to the side, looking down at his prosthetic shoe.

Father Patterson turned and started off by thanking me for everything I had done for the past few weeks and got right to the point. "We're sorry Tommy, but we won't be inviting you back for our next class in the fall," he stated.

"Why?" I stammered incredulously.

At this point, Brother Leonardo stood as if on cue, and started to read a list of infractions from a piece of paper.

"Count one: Improper use of a clerical collar, in order to receive a ten percent discount for the purchase of alcohol.

"Count two: corrupting the morals of seminarians by gambling via an all-night card game, carried out in the main dorm last Saturday night.

"Count three," Brother Leonardo continued, a smirk creeping across his face, "swapping out the chapel's acoustic guitars and organ for two new electric Fender guitars and a Marshall amp at Jack's Music Store.

"Count four: intentionally removing a third of the Bingo numbers in the tumbler, so as to defraud the bingo customers."

Feeling cornered and flushed now, I felt my mouth go dry as I addressed Father Patterson. "Yes, I did all those things, but certainly not out of any malicious intent. I figured some of the parents would want a few cold ones at the cookout and as far as the Bingo game went…"

"SILENCE!" Father Patterson bellowed at me, waving off my meritless excuses. He expressed his grave disappointment in me and told me I had violated his trust. His words echoed harsh but true, and he let them hang in the air until I felt ashamed, embarrassed and small. He told me to gather my belongings and to leave immediately. He coldly shook my hand, turned his back on me and began gazing out the large window again. As crestfallen as I felt, I thanked him for the opportunity, said my "goodbyes" and headed for home.

After what felt like going through the five stages of a death sentence, I tried to think about Jackie's and Nora's upcoming wedding to brighten my mood. When I got home, dad was the only one there. He had just finished grocery shopping and was sticking the food receipt tape, which no one ever read, on the fridge door. After explaining what had happened, he told me to try to find a silver lining in all of this, and the more patronizing he became, the better I started to feel.

I called Sears back and as luck would have it, my order picker's position hadn't been filled yet. They were willing to give me my old job back. Next, I called Carla, who initially didn't show me much sympathy after I told her how I had washed out of the program. At first, she was a little standoffish, but after a few minutes of chatting she couldn't suppress her optimistic nature any longer. I apologized for treating her as badly as I had and acting like a jerk and she graciously forgave me.

Jackie arrived home from work and started to fill me in on the wedding arrangements. Seems him and Nora had already lined up the hall, caterer, invitations, flowers, photographer, limo, and the cake.

"Who's providing the music?" I inquired.

"Little Dan Teehan and his Irish Show Band," he said.

"Wow, that's a nine-piece band, four-horn section included," I gushed. "Yep," Jackie bragged. "Nora's uncle Frank is related to Little Dan, and he gave us the date and a ten percent discount, too." "Is there anything I can do?" I asked.

"Two things," Jackie replied. "First, tell me you will do me the honor of being my best man. And secondly, can you get us a church and a priest to officiate?"

"Jeez," I cried. "How much longer were you going to wait on the priest and church?"

"I figured with your newfound connections in the seminary, it would be a cinch."

"Well," I began, "the wedding is still a couple of months away. I think I can make it all happen. I just want to wait a week or two before I ask him."

"Ask who?" Jackie inquired. "Father Patterson," I said.

Two weeks to the day after I left the seminary, I was standing once again before its large, arched, oak doors. I knocked, Brother Leonardo appeared, and asked me the nature of my visit. I said I was there on personal business to see Father Patterson. He brought me to the prefect's office and let me in. Father Patterson seemed glad to see me and asked, "Isn't anyone ever home at your house? I've been trying to reach you for over a week."

"We do all work in the day," I said. "Why did you want to contact me?" "St. Francis will be conducting classes soon for men of good faith interested in becoming deacons, and I thought you would be a good fit," Father said.

"What's a deacon do?" I asked.

"Deacons are keepers of the faith, whereas priests are teachers of the faith. Deacons assist in various parish activities at the pastor's discretion. They can prepare the church for holy mass, serve as ushers, and help around the parish in any number of ways."

"Helping out on Bingo Night?" I asked.

"Well, yes, helping out on Bingo Night. Although in your case, Tommy, I think we'll be having you sell coffee and donuts as opposed to calling the games," he admonished.

"Touché, Father. I would be thrilled and honored to serve in any capacity the parish saw fit." I apologized to him for all the nonsense and bullshit I had caused him during my two weeks probation. Father looked at me paternally as if I were the prodigal son returning home, smiled warmly and stated, "I always knew you had a good heart Tommy, if somewhat...misplaced. But what type of priest would I be if I couldn't exhibit forgiveness and extend second chances, my son? What type, indeed?"

I asked him if St. Francis Church could serve as the site for my brother's wedding and if he would marry the couple. After confirming that he and the church were both available for duty for the date in question, I asked him how he knew about all the infractions I had committed during my probationary period. He looked over at

Brother Leonardo who was sheepishly looking down at his prosthetic shoe again and said, "Let's just say that the walls have ears, and leave it at that."

I filled out the paperwork for the deacon program and handed it back. Prior to heading home, I asked Father if he had time to tell me the parable of the two boats that moved but didn't move, again.

"Perhaps later, Tommy. Right now I have a previous engagement. I'll give you a call later to go over any last minute details for the wedding."

By the day of the wedding everything was running like clockwork. I was dating Carla again, back at Sears picking orders, and I was being enrolled into the deacon's program at the seminary. Life was grand indeed.

When the big day finally arrived, the house was buzzing with excitement. My three younger brothers were serving as ushers. Carla was the maid of honor, and a few of Nora's cousins were going to be bridesmaids. The whole family looked great, even gramps, who seemed to be absorbing the whole atmosphere. The other quirky thing about gramps was that whenever mom cooked now, all he wanted to eat was fish sticks and lima beans, even for breakfast.

Jeez, the only issue at all that day was when dad kept muttering, "Shit and two is six," as he fiddled with his tux tie.

Speaking of which, the boys down at Tux Deluxe had really outdone themselves with our outfits. They suited us up in jet-black jackets with matching tight trousers that flared at the bottom. The light lavender shirts were ruffled down the middle over the buttons with billowy sleeves that made them look like pirate shirts. The icing on the cake was the offsetting, sparkling, silvery vest with a rounded cutout that started at the nipple and ran down to and around the navel.

The patent leather shoes had a blinding, glossy shine on them, only mine were one size too small lengthwise, and definitely too tight widthwise. I foolishly neglected to try them on after I picked them up, and they had obviously given me the wrong ones. *It's too late now,* I thought.

Father Patterson gave a beautiful service, and in his homily he used an analogy of a bride and a groom to the church and Christ and all the complementary blessings that accompany such a union. Following Mass, the wedding party took an open tram to the reception while the one hundred and fifty guests followed in their own vehicles.

After the wedding pictures were taken, we all headed into the main hall with the other guests for a family-style dinner of roast beef and vegetables. Everyone seemed to enjoy the meal except for gramps, who we found in the kitchen badgering the caterer about not having fish sticks and lima beans on the menu.

After dinner, when all the preliminaries involving garter belts and first dances were over, everyone started to break off into smaller cliques around the tables. Carla and I broke off from the head table to sit with friends. At one point, Vito grabbed the gallon of Seagram's VO, which served as the table's centerpiece, turned to his girlfriend Maria and drunkenly teased her that he had found her misplaced drink.

On a prearranged signal with the band, the ushers and about a dozen preselected male friends all got on the dance floor as the first few strains of the *'Electric Slide'* came from the bandstand. The females were politely dissuaded from joining in for this one song, in an attempt to get a few laughs from the crowd. By this stage, aided in part by an open bar, most inhibitions were long gone, and the dance floor remained filled for the rest of the night.

At one point near the end of the evening, I was sitting with Carla and she was prodding me about "our future." Because we sat beside one another instead of facing each other, I was able to discreetly stick the rounded end of a spoon in my right eye without her seeing me— sort of like using the muscles around the eye to hold a monocle in place. She didn't laugh when I turned to face her in the middle of such a serious conversation.

A few moments later, the band had a prearranged announcement to make. "Could everyone please clear the dance floor, and could Tommy McCauley please come to the bandstand?" By now I had my tux jacket off as I approached bandleader, Dan Teehan, who handed me a pencil-thin microphone with a cord that must have extended twenty feet. I walked out to the middle of the empty dance floor as Dan counted off to four, then pointed at his horn section who began to play the opening brass bars to the Tom Jones hit, *'Help Yourself.'*

"Ba ba ba bump, ba bump ba baaa ... Ba ba ba bump ba bump ba baaa." Bolstered by the effects of an open bar and feeling totally energized and in command, I launched into my song on time, on key and on target. Now the full force of the band was in play, the guitars, organ, drums and the horns... those glorious horns. I segued from the verse to the chorus back to the verse in seamless transitions that climaxed with my uncanny ability to replicate every one of Mr. Jones's manic dance moves to perfection. I poised my right arm over my head and let it crash down in perfect synch with every lyric and note in a Pete Townsendesque windmill motion.

The *Billboard 100* gods must have been smiling down on me that night as my jerky Tom Jones head tosses and hip thrusts had the audience doing double takes. It was a mini *tour de force* that combined choreography, voice, and instrument perfection with a double shot of VO and karma.

I finished the song and the crowd, which had formed a large circle, started to close in on me. They let out a roar of approval and moved in around me offering congratulations and back slaps all around. After the furor died down, I went to my table and switched off my tight-fitting tux shoes for a pair of black sneakers I had brought along. Dan Teehan stepped up to the mike, encouraged the crowd to give me another round of applause, and announced the last dance of the night.

Jackie and Nora had changed into their street clothes and started dancing to the Ann Murray wedding favorite, *'May I Have This Dance.'*

The crowd formed a tight circle around the newlyweds and began to gently sway in time to the song. At the conclusion of the dance, the hall lights went up as Carla and I started to leave the building with other small groups of revelers.

Right before we exited the hall, Carla noticed I was wearing sneakers and asked me where my tux shoes were. I turned around to the table where I had left them, and saw my old boyhood pal Vito loitering nearby. I shouted to him, *"Vito, Get le scarpe, Get le scarpe!"*

Carla turned to me and asked, "What does that mean?"

I smiled at her and said, "That's Italian for *'Get my shoes!'* Everybody knows that."

Confessions Of A Non-Best-Selling Author

My overnight at the Convention Center started out about as uneventful as any other shift I had pulled over the past few weeks. I was one month retired from the post office, in a funky college section of Boston called Allston, situated nearly dead center between Boston College and crosstown rival Boston University.

Allston is primarily made up of a multi-grain mix of people of every stripe, with a corresponding number of restaurants, thrift stores and head shops to satisfy every eclectic taste there.

The student population falls right in line with the number of absentee landlords who spend their hours ignoring their properties while gouging the parents of students who dwell in the hovels dotting the roads between Brighton Avenue and Cambridge Street.

I spent my first eleven years there, humping mail to a largely invisible base of postal customers, due to class schedules and/or debilitating hangovers from all night keggers. I then morphed into a front-line supervisor over the next seventeen years, recording junk mail volumes and generating reams of redundant reports for the man. Now sixty, I was ready to cut my workload in half.

With my twenty-eight years of federal service, plus another twelve years performing non-essential work as a magnetic tape librarian for a large Boston bank, I was now officially semi-retired. I seamlessly took my forty years of career know-how and life experiences and parlayed it into a part-time gig pulling security at the

Boston Convention Center. I'm not ashamed to mention that I blew away the three talking heads who made up the interview committee, although I thought their number was a tad excessive for a job that paid a lousy twelve bucks an hour.

About three weeks after my appointment to the BCC, I reconnected through social media with a boyhood friend named Bill L. whom I hadn't had contact with in some thirty-odd years. We readily agreed to meet in Boston's redeveloped Seaport District over calamari, fish tacos, and three decades of catching up, washed down by pitchers of lager. Aside from another twenty or so pounds added to our frames and some grey hair, we looked pretty much as we did in the go-go eighties.

We weren't together twenty minutes before we were picking up old verbal queues and finishing each other's sentences, like we never missed a beat. Being a journalist, I knew Bill L. had worked for the *Cape Cod Times* before taking similar positions in and around Newport News, Virginia and the newspapers serving the Finger Lakes region in New York. I also knew his timeline ran somewhere between the late seventies to the early eighties covering these rags, before he decided to transition his skill set to New York City.

Bill L. noshed on his taco, cleared his throat and started to explain how, once in the city, he had quickly segued from print media to television and had never looked back. Once he got his foot in the door, he began writing content for daytime talk shows for the likes of Ricki Lake and Geraldo Rivera. He had also pitched in writing some of those corny double- entendres Robin Leach was so fond of using on his *Lifestyles of the Rich and Famous* program.

Before long, he was producing segments for these shows, all the while absorbing every nuance and trick of the trade. He schooled himself in everything from audio prep and video editing to green screens and post production. Armed with this knowledge and after kicking around the Big Apple for some dozen years, he decided to return home to Boston, taking a television job at Channel 5, the largest market in New England.

Snagging the last taco and taking a long pull on his beer, Bill L. went on to note he had since left Channel 5. He got his degree in Television Production, teaches courses on the subject at Northeastern as a tenured professor, lectures at colleges in L.A. and Beijing, has his own animation studio and also co-hosts a weekly podcast for a hobby.

Then he asked me what I've been up to.

I sheepishly replied that when I was previously employed supervising the efficient management of workhours vs. workloads for a bloated, near bankrupt bureaucracy, I could also be found coaching third base for my granddaughter's 8th grade softball team.

We polished off another pitcher, paid our check and made plans to get together again before social security became insolvent.

The next night at four a.m. I was sitting in a 12 x 15-foot breakroom, in a hall that had the capacity to hold six football fields. I was wearing a cheap, baggy, polyester security uniform, staring at my A&W beverage and a dried-up bologna sandwich. Pissa!

My dark mood turned more morose as I ruminated over the gargantuan contrasts between Bill L's career trajectory and mine. I realized it was a tough pill to swallow comparing two careers so diametrically opposite one another.

Lost in thought, I rewound a 16-millimeter visual of my life, trying to ferret out my most momentous decisions that had had the greatest impact on my existence. I knew if I didn't make a quick decision regarding my current state of mind, the only place I would ever find my self-respect would be at the bottom of a root beer bottle, wallowing in self-pity. I was finally taking a lifetime inventory of regrettable decisions and squared them against my lamentable reality.

Where, I wondered, *was my potential? Where had…my life gone?*

After brainstorming thirty minutes of my lunch break away, and taking the full measure of my talents, I came to one unanimous conclusion: I'd write a book. A humorous book! And why not? I like humor and I like words. It was a natural fit. Thinking back on the comedic chops my pop possessed, I recalled some of the more acerbic witticisms he would scribble on my paper lunch bags when I was still in high school. A few of his classics included, "Get a Haircut!" "Get a Job!" and my favorite, "Don't Come Home!" which he probably got the most mileage out of.

Buoyed with a renewed sense of purpose and a steely determination to leave my mark, I wolfed down the rest of my sandwich and headed over to Hall B to activate escalators that would help usher in thousands of Pokémon zealots for the center's largest Anime Convention later that morning.

I suppose my preoccupation with an invigorating resolve to pen the next Runyonesque tome of short stories precluded me from noticing that I had mistakenly keyed all the escalators in the "up" position.

This miscue created a human logjam of epic proportions for the lanyard clad, animation fanatics, delaying the shows 9 a.m. opening by half an hour. My "gross and willful negligence," cited on my "Letter of Warning" per BCC management, would now blemish my Official Personal File in time memoriam.

Despite this setback, I remained steadfast in my quest to write my first book. The fact that writing prolific humor wasn't offered in the *For Dummies* series was my first obstacle. When I drilled down deeper about such an undertaking, my self-doubt kicked in, sucker-punching my confidence in the face.

Realistically, what did I know about themes, plotlines and protagonists?

How would I weave symbolism into my tales or find my literary voice?

I was starting to feel that following hot dog king Joey Chestnut into a public restroom on July 5th would have been an easier endeavor.

I caught myself and vowed that I wouldn't allow a self-defeating attitude to define me. Instead, for inspiration, I concentrated on a myriad of favored authors over past generations. I was seeking mirth masters and wordsmiths of the first order. My heroes ran the gamut from the Marx Brother's Svengali, S.J. Perelman to Seinfeld savant, Larry David, and everyone in between. Yet, I always came back to John Hughes. I recalled his epic tale '*Vacation 58*', featured in a long-lost copy of *National Lampoon*, and googled it to reread this mini masterpiece once again.

I gleaned two stylistic elements from this brilliant narrative: First, his wonderful progression of comical sequences that build from one scene to the next, and second: his ability to write as economically as possible. Mr. Hughes was the antithesis of the wordy and the surplus sentence. Now that I had an influential writing template, I focused my energies on a premise.

Since I had nothing in the way of a catchy beginning, a spellbinding middle or a compelling ending, I gave way to a convoluting logic that had me jotting down funny stories, half-truths and quirky anecdotes from my youth.

After a month of scrawling these snippets into a notebook, I was satisfied that I had enough material to start. Aided by a MacBook Pro, I began stringing phrases together until they blossomed from paragraphs into pages and numbered sixty-five. I estimated spending two to three hours on each page, which allowed for multiple drafts, edits and revisions.

When I was done, I christened it, *Dance of the Deacon.* Technically, it was a novella that captured a ten-year stretch in my life, covering everything from family vacations to young love to a flirtation with joining the priesthood. The accent was decidedly on absurdist humor.

In rapid succession, I composed four more short stories. One was a dream-like tale where three somewhat reluctant authors appear to me, tasked with tutoring me on the finer aspects of the arts and letters. My next short had me reminiscing about taking an office crush to a Rolling Stones concert that went south in no time flat. I then wrote a pocket piece of an imagined conversation that a father and son might conceivably have after a thirty-year absence.

Finally, I wrote a historical fiction story about a sports reporter covering the connection between Calvin Coolidge, pitcher Walter Johnson and the '24 Washington Senators. The entire literary exercise clocked in at around one hundred pages.

I had my offing professionally proof-read, corrected and edited by a publisher at no small cost. I did however, balk at my editor's full book package deal, which I found cost prohibitive. I read up on how to self-publish on Amazon with no up-front costs and elected to run with their e-reader publishing program on Kindle.

Next on the agenda was finding a suitable title and pen name. Initially, I considered *Fifty Shades of Funny,* but quickly figured readers might find it disingenuous where none of the stories contained any sex, let alone bondage scenes.

Focusing back on a title that conveyed humor and a sprinkle of surrealism, I settled on, *Hey Mom, the Recliner Fell on Dad Again!* It doesn't exactly roll off the tongue, but it was dubbed in the same vein as Tim Allen's *Don't Stand Too Close to a Naked Man!* Similar pretense.

Turning to pseudonyms, I briefly toyed with using Tommy Higgins Clark as a moniker, until my wife convinced me that such a name would likely generate an avalanche of "cease and desist" letters from the law offices of Simon and Schuster. I caved and went with my own handle.

When I read deeper into the Amazon Kindle program, I found out they were churning out one million titles per year. When I ran the math, I estimated that with 330 million people in the country,

I was roughly 1 in 330. When I subtracted another 230 million from the ranks because they were either too young, too feeble, or too disinclined to write, I found myself at about 1 in 100. Psychologically, the panache of being published started to erode.

Despite these depressing numbers, Amazon does allow authors to set their own prices and is willing to let writers keep up to seventy percent, for every title downloaded. I priced my e-reader on Kindle for a measly $2.99 in the hopes that its puny price would attract a larger audience. After completing a three-page online questionnaire, answering generic questions about the book, I pressed the submit button. Less than one day later, *Hey Mom, the Recliner Fell on Dad Again!* was available to my adoring public.

When the book did flash, I awarded myself the honor of being the first one to download it. Unfortunately, I had only quickly skimmed the contents before announcing to the Facebook world that I had indeed arrived as a published author. Feeling accomplished, a bit smug and ready to start watching the royalties roll in, I settled into my easy chair, grabbed my Kindle and nearly chocked on my chicken loaf sandwich to realize my creation was chock full of errors, typos, and mispunctuations. Talk about rookie mistakes.

I went back into my Amazon account, deleted my "live" book, and contacted Word-to-Kindle. They're a company that runs a program that formats Word Docx to an e-reader, and corrects any errors, making one's manuscript letter perfect. The only drawback was, it took a month to get the sanitized version back. After going "live" again, I made another gross miscalculation in assuming my 247 Facebook friends would translate into 247 purchases. Although they weren't buying my product, they were pretty generous with the number of likes and smiley-faced emojis they were messaging me back with.

After a few months shilling on FB and all the groups I belonged to, my account only tallied thirty-five downloads, earning me the princely sum of seventy dollars. My next strategy was to get some word-of-mouth traction by giving my life's story away for free through Amazon ads. In the five days that the promotion ran, I garnered another seventy sales. (Actually, non-sales since it was free.)

I was starting to think that the chances of snagging a Green Jacket at Augusta National would have been more likely than making another sale. Another minor setback hit me when I noticed that by keying in the first two words of my title on Amazon books, the default would go straight to comedian Louie Anderson's book, *Hey Mom, Stories For My Mother, But You Can Read Them Too!* Jeez, this title was as bad as mine. To counter comedian Louie Anderson's blatant intrusion, I considered swapping out the "Hey Mom" part in my title for "Hey Grandma," in the belief it would pop right alongside Paul McCartney's children's book, *Hey Grandude!* Sorry comedian Louie Anderson, but when it comes to book sales and cachet, I'm throwing my lot in with the ex-Beatle. Alas, too late, the dye had been cast.

My next plan was to enter my shorts into several reputable writing contests and let the book rise or fall on its own literary merits. After a year of reading rejection e-mails that were populating my inbox, I finally tasted a smidgen of success. My book placed as Finalist in the 2019 Faulkner-Wisdom Competition. Winners of the various categories would be flown to New Orleans, ensconced in a French Quarter hotel, and then awarded their prize in an ancient Ursuline convent by the Faulkner Society.

I daydreamed of attending the ceremony, being feted and magnanimously submitting myself to the autograph and Q and A sessions with grace, wit and charm. I would then Uber back to my Bourbon Street hotel, tossing leftover beads and trinkets from Mardi Gras to the minions in the street below before giving a final limp-wristed papal wave, and retiring for the night. Then I woke up!

Placing as a Finalist was indeed the critical high-water mark for *Hey Mom, the Recliner Fell on Dad Again!* Although this Boomer still keeps finding that pesky copy and paste command vexing, it was still a project filled with self-discovery and satisfaction.

How could it not be? With mentors like Bill L. John Hughes and even comedian Louie Anderson pioneering the way for a security guard with a dream in his heart and a walkie-talkie in his pants, the good fight would continue to be fought, and one day God willing, would be won.

* * *

Dear reader, if you enjoyed this book, please consider giving it a short review or a rating on the book's Amazon page.

Thank you, Tom McKenna